THE
BLIND
Accordionist

Also by C. D. Rose

The Biographical Dictionary of Literary Failure

Who's Who When Everyone Is Someone Else

THE
BLIND
Accordionist

NINE STORIES BY MAXIM GUYAVITCH

C.D. ROSE

MELVILLE HOUSE
BROOKLYN · LONDON

The Blind Accordionist

Melville House Publishing
46 John Street
Brooklyn, NY 11201
and
Melville House UK
Suite 2000
16/18 Woodford Road
London E7 0HA

mhpbooks.com
@melvillehouse

ISBN: 978-1-61219-917-7
ISBN: 978-1-61219-918-4 (eBook)

Library of Congress Control Number: 2021932785

Designed by Amy King

Printed in the United States of America
10 9 8 7 6 5 4 3 2 1
A catalog record for this book is available from the Library of Congress

CONTENTS

♦ ♠ ♥ ♣

INTRODUCTION

MAXIM GUYAVITCH WAS born in Galicia in 1882. Or Dalmatia in 1894. Or perhaps in Moldavia, or maybe that's Moravia, in 1888, or '89, or '90.

He was an orphan who joined the army in order to save himself from destitution; the only son of a neglectful bourgeois family; an inveterate gambler; the greatest writer you have never heard of; a thief; someone with a far more respectable career as something other than a writer who used a pseudonym to publish their work; an itinerant pianist; a serial dissident; a man obsessed with pears. Opinions vary. Theories proliferate. "He" may actually have been a collective of writers, all for one reason or another anxious to hide their true identities. He may never have existed at all.

Truth is, no one knows much about Maxim Guyavitch.

What we can be sure of: Stories under his name began to appear in small magazines in various countries and various languages in the early twentieth century. There were only ever nine of them. Sometime in the early 1930s, they stopped.

What we can't be sure of: anything else.

The stories were later collected and published in German, Czech, Polish, French, Russian, English, Hungarian, and various other languages in editions ranging from leather-bound, gold-embossed volumes destined for private libraries to knock-offs made of cigarette paper and glue to be flogged at railway station stalls and newspaper kiosks. Few editions ever sold more than a handful of copies, and, fairly rapidly, they dropped out of print, then memory.

If you look carefully and study the minutiae of publishers' catalogues, conference proceedings, and literary tittle-tattle, you may from time to time see his name surface, and the stories, too, as they are rediscovered, then reforgotten. In the book world undergrowth, a small para-industry has flourished, samizdat versions of the stories have been circulated, and dubious new ones have emerged and, their authorship contested, sunk. Minor academics at major universities and major academics at minor universities have specialised. Letters have been written. Websites with improbable names, immune to search engines, still exist. His name was—and still is—whispered knowingly, as though uttering it might show membership in a certain group, though his work has been rarely read.

A few years ago, the modest success of the publication of a series of my lectures[1] created another small ripple of interest in Guyavitch and his work, and I was invited to edit a new edition of his *Nine Stories*.

---

1 *Who's Who When Everyone Is Someone Else*, Melville House, Brooklyn and London, 2018

The task was far from a simple one. The texts that exist are now difficult to come by, often corrupt, and usually conflicting. The edition I have put together—the book you hold in your hands or have laid flat on your table before you right now—may infuriate purists, pedants, and Pharisees, but I care little. Others may consider my choices merely idiosyncratic. For example, I have not included the story "Little Eli's Shoes," as I believe it of dubious authenticity and inferior quality, but I *have* included "Dead Johann," refusing to accept the notion that it is somehow "cursed."[2] I have arranged them in what I believe to be chronological order of production, noting the stylistic, thematic, and—I believe—personal development from "The Card Players" as far as "The Visitors." In short, this is, I believe, the edition Guyavitch's work deserves.

But enough. I do not wish to detain you further with distraction from the stories themselves. To those of you who already know Guyavitch, I hope you will again experience the wonder of reading these tales, as if for the first time. To those of you new to this curious, unsettling, beguiling writer, read on, and read carefully, for you may never return.

---

2 Though neither am I convinced by the suggestion that it is, in fact, the key to this enigmatic collection of work.

A BRIEF NOTE ON
THE TRANSLATION

WHETHER AN ART, a science, or a craft, literary translation has been variously compared to a pane of glass, a bridge, a woman, a string quartet playing a piano sonata, a kiss through a blanket, and a mule. It has been described as an ongoing contradiction, an act of intimacy, an act of surrender, an act of espionage, a necessary act of barbarism, and the art of failure.

Arguments rage (*rage!*) over target versus source, soundness versus shapeliness, and fidelity versus licence. Should a translation be correct or comely, deforming or reforming, expressive or instrumental, faithful or free? Some speak of the joys of corruption, others of the pleasure of the pure. Should footnotes pile up at the bottom of the page, or should the translated text fend for itself? A translator may always be tempted to polish, to rephrase, to rewrite, even to stray—while still remaining faithful. But faithful to what? What source text is ever pure? What manuscript does not bear pentimenti and erasures, second, third, and fourth thoughts? What book has not passed through the hands of editors, proofreaders, typesetters, advance readers, and the marketing department?

I once knew someone (who was an idiot) who claimed they would never read a work in translation, as it was not authentic. But there is no authentic text, no original. There are only ever versions of some Platonic form, echoes with no source. That is all we are.

I have faith. Translators, I believe, are magi, silver-tongued shapeshifters deftly slipping from one language to another. They are illuminators, curators, bearers, blessed and cursed to be forever between two (or three, or four) cultures and languages. Without translators, we would not be able to exist.

It is unclear what language Guyavitch wrote in—no autograph manuscripts survive—and we may be fairly certain that he had no mother tongue but was born into a capacious family of languages. The work you have here has been collated from a number of different editions, each one in turn disputed or possibly corrupt, and in many cases, no original translator was named. Put simply: funds available for this translation were scarce, so I have done the best job I could.

Walter Benjamin wrote that "all great texts contain their potential translation between the lines," and this is the case here. All life is between the lines; all is potential.

Any infelicities and inconsistencies here are my own. All other errors are volitional, and therefore portals of discovery.

C.D.R.

THE CARD
PLAYERS

——— ♦ ♠ ♥ ♣ ———

CHRISTMAS HAD PASSED, and though the bottles of pear champagne had been opened and drunk, January was reluctant to arrive. Snow, ice, and frost had slowed not only passage into or out of the town, but the very days themselves. At this sink of the year, the cold could crack bones. These days—when the light was starting to fight back but the darkness still won—inspired little desire to celebrate; everyone waited for the year to show itself before welcoming it. Beginnings to the year are rarely auspicious— it is only humanity, after all, that has chosen to mark them thus. Nature cares little, as it has neither ending nor beginning.

Some mornings—like this one—the very air seemed ice itself, each breath enough to freeze the tissue that lined a man's lungs. The light hung ashen and sluggish, thick and slow. The river that curled around the town had grown solid enough to build a railway on. Ice ruled the land.

And yet, this gelid day had been warmed by a rumour stewing, softening the bite of the chill and perfuming the town with its potent smell of possibility.

The Marquis went out at five, as the Marquis did, but today Eva and Ada had listened carefully, knowing the soft thud of each footfall, the creak of every floorboard, and the scrape of every opening drawer well enough to be able to envision him carefully trimming his moustache, slipping the small compact mirror into his right glove, then choosing his shiniest shoes to wear under his felt overboots. He came down (they scurried), then ate nothing but a slice of black bread with white cheese and requested only a light broth for supper on his return.

The rumour was true.

Tonight, there was to be a game.

Ada and Eva watched the Marquis head down the path and, once convinced he was out of eye and earshot, ran upstairs to change.

"The red?" asked Eva.

"No, the green," replied Ada.

"The fox fur?"

"The sable."

"Shoes?"

"Boots."

Once painted, shod, coated, scarved, and furred, they opened their front door.

"Brass monkey," said Eva.

"Frog's tail," said Ada.

"The Devil's shoulder," said Eva.

"Witch's tit," said Ada, and they set out.

They passed the cinnamon shop and the coral merchant, the seller of tallow candles and the importer of damasks. The baker had begun selling off the morning's now-stale loaves, the printer had hushed his press. Behind the banked-up snow and the spaces of the silence, the rumour had taken flesh, begun to crawl, then to walk as fast as the small crowd now gathering around Eva and Ada, following the Marquis at a distance ample enough to consider themselves unseen. Peter and Johann cracked their knuckles, ready to pick pockets; the cartographer rolled his maps; Grasso carried up bottles of pear brandy from the cellar and stoked the fires. In the back room of the Golden Lion, a man sat with his notebook, frantically trying to record everything that was happening—everything, that is, as far as he knew or understood it, and quite possibly just making a lot of it up.

The town had no railway, but its arrival had once been promised, and in anticipation of that day a hotel had been built and popularly named the Station Hotel, and it was there, at this very moment, that a man with hunched shoulders and a bent nose wearing a stiff black suit and an unfashionable, wing-collared shirt, neither warm enough for the scouringly cold weather, walked down the stairs, across the lobby, and onto the street.

Even though evening was already cowling the narrow streets, the light seemed unexpected to him, and from his breast pocket he produced a pair of dark-tinted, oval-lensed glasses, which he carefully rested on the bridge of his nose and would leave there for the rest of the evening.

From behind these glasses, he looked around a moment; then he struck out, his boots clacking on the stone flags, then thudding on the board pavement as he turned off the square and made decisively for the knot of old streets in the town centre. On the corner where the alleys untangled and the main street began, he saw a group of people huddled in a close circle. Believing them to be warming their hands at a fire and now himself feeling the cold, he walked over to join them, but as he grew closer, the small crowd dispersed like leaves floating in a teacup, and he discovered there was no fire, and that they were gathered around nothing at all.

He feigned composure, adjusted his jacket against the cold, and carried on his way, vaguely aware of the crowd reforming behind him. The crowd, indeed, turned their heads to observe his progress. They muttered to themselves and nodded to each other. It was true: He was making for the Golden Lion. Not only was there to be a game this evening, the Galician had come to play.

The Marquis was the first at table. The Marquis was always the first at table. There was no reason for this, no rule except the unwritten one: if the Marquis wasn't first at table, the evening's game couldn't begin. As the Marquis took his seat, removing his overcoat and felt boots, the Galician was making his way down Golden Lion Street. As the Marquis broke a fresh pack of cards, the Galician was heaving open the heavy door into the saloon and pulling back the insulating curtain behind it. As the Marquis ordered a pear brandy, the Galician was brushing snow from his unsuitable shoes. As the Marquis sipped his brandy, the Galician walked into the back room of the Golden Lion Inn.

The game could begin.

The crowd swelled and bobbed. Ada and Eva were already there. Although they had left after the Marquis, their skill in navigating the slippery roads matched with their intention not to miss a second of the evening's adventure and led them to arrive before the Marquis. Despite the external chill, the fierce stove soon made the room uncomfortably hot, and many of the women removed their furs as more people (Peter and Johann, the cartographer's wife, the cinnamon seller) also pushed their way into the back room of the inn. Klug even brought the dog who he swore could talk, though no one had ever heard it do so. Two men who have no part in the story stood shoulder to shoulder in matching grey overcoats.

A chair was found for their visitor, and the crowd, anxious to know more about the newcomer, attempted to engage him in conversation.

"Have you visited our town before?" they asked him, but the Galician shook his head.

"Not that I remember," he replied.

"How do you know of the game?" they asked.

"Everyone knows about the game," he replied. No one asked who "everyone" was, each of them believing it to be themselves, and indeed, they did all know about the game, even if they did not know quite where it had come from.

The game, some said, was part of the Trick-Taking family, related to Euchre; similar, in its way, to Skat, Clabber, or Juckerspiel. Others claimed it was a branch of the Cuckoo group of

Draw-and-Discard, and more akin to Bester Bube or Krypka-sino, while others saw it as a piece of Schafkopf, like Spitzer or Kierki, or even a Partition game, like Chor Voli or Hazari. Still others considered it a variant of the classic Vying games, a distant cousin of Poker, Brag, Bouillotte, or Ferbli. The *chemin de fer* variation of Baccarat was also often cited. Discussions regarding the game's ancestry were as lengthy, complex, and passionate as the game itself. There was no right, no wrong, no reason. No one knew. The game was what it was.

"Surely," thought the crowd, "the Galician has an ancestor here. How else could he know about the game?" No one claimed to be related to the Galician, though Karm believed his uncle had once visited the region.

No stranger had come to play the game for as long as anyone could remember. The crowd speculated: the Galician, surely, was a millionaire come in hugger-mugger to buy up cheap land, or finally to bring the railway to town; the Galician was the illegitimate child of a shamed but unnamed local come to claim his rightful inheritance, or, at least, to demand recognition from his errant sire; the Galician was a spurned lover pulled by the magnetic force of jealousy; a lone traveller who had lost his way; an imperial spy; a nihilist anarchist; a cunning plotter come to destabilise everything everyone had ever known or would ever know. The Galician, it was said, wasn't even Galician.

The Galician said nothing.

(The speculation, however, fluttered around the Marquis's ears, making him uncomfortable, as it was known too that the

Marquis wasn't actually a Marquis, though he had been called so ever since anyone could remember. No one knew why, not even Ada and Eva.)

Although no one knew who the Galician was, he had come to play, and on this the rules were clear: the table was open, anyone was welcome to take their seat, and this the Galician did.

The work of the night awaited.

The crowd pointed out that there was no extra chair. The Marquis had a chair, the Galician seated opposite him had a chair, but there was no empty chair. One of the rules of the game (though whether it was a rule or merely tradition wasn't certain) was that one empty chair should always be present at the table. Should someone else, a guest uninvited or unexpected, a passing stranger, even, wish to take part in the dealing, shuffling, exchanging, and placing of the cards, they would always be welcomed. Stray drinkers stuck in the saloon were displaced as a chair was liberated and passed into the crowded back room, then given to the card players.

Another round of drinks was poured, though the Galician declined the offer of pear brandy and said he would prefer linden tea. Grasso had his wife prepare a pot of linden tea.

They were almost ready to make the toast that would signal the opening of the evening's game, but the tea was still too hot. They waited for the tea to cool.

While they waited for the tea to cool, the Marquis reshuffled two packs of cards, one French, the other Neapolitan. As the host, he would open the evening's play, though—it was said—he could, as a courtesy, ask the Galician to lay the welcoming card, but this was most improbable.

Someone could have consulted a rule book, but there was no rule book.

The game had its rules, but the rules were unwritten. Everything was precedent, tradition. Each precedent had, perhaps, begun as a cheat, or a challenge. No group had ever formally sat and ratified changes to the game. The rules were like the life-sized map of the town held in the Cartographer's shop: no one had ever seen it; all believed in its existence, apocryphal as it may be.

The game had been played in the town for many years, though no one knew how many. The game had not always been played in the back bar of the Golden Lion. Over the years, the game had moved from inn to tavern to the storeroom of the baker to the salon of the big house at the edge of town, and then back again around this circuit. The game had been played in the town square, under hedges, in fields, and at one point it was said that the game was being played only by two men in a ditch.

Different traditions related that the game dated back to when a bride was gambled, or children auctioned, or to the founding of the town itself by a man who had had to sell all his land. The game had begun so long ago no one could quite remember when it had begun, or where, or how, or why.

"Before we begin," said the Galician, "may I ask a question?"

The Marquis assented; the crowd cocked its ear.

"Would it be possible," he asked, "to add my own pack?"

Although there had been many iterations of the game, it was— as far as anyone knew—always played with at least two packs of cards, and sometimes as many as nine. French and Neapolitan were standard, Latin and Swiss sometimes used, even Silesian or Sicilian, and very occasionally Tarot.

The request baffled the crowd. The polyphonic unwritten rules were consulted: the crowd debated; opinions varied.

Cheating, Klug reminded everyone, was not unheard of in the game. There were many modes of cheating, Karm asserted, some of which, over the years, had come to be accepted as acceptable modes of play. The Marquis himself had been known to cheat, had even admitted it, only a little, only ever slightly, but he was able to justify himself: it was, he claimed, his way of righting the balance of the world, of taking action against an unjust universe. He had, he said, been cheated against on several occasions (both large and small), but had—in those cases—never taken any revenge nor caused any scene nor publicly questioned anyone's honour. He had merely decided, in turn, to cheat *back*. Such was the world, said the Marquis. Cheating could happen, but cheating had to be regulated. The Galician could certainly propose a new pack, but the pack would have to be inspected.

It was set to be a long evening. Food supplies were called for: the soup was stirred, the stale bread dampened and put back in the relit oven. Grasso carted up more pear brandy from his cellar. Link boys, their buckets of fire hanging on the ends of their poles, would be needed to guide the drunks home.

A committee (Grasso, Klug and Karm, Johann and Peter) hastily assembled, abetted by the others, each with their own theory: the Galician was going to play a double, introduce an extra to the pack, one more card, thus disturbing the game's precise possibilities of combinations of variants. According to the rules, each card should have its twin, although the twin card was not necessarily identical. But if the card were, in turn, marked in some way (a dog-ear, a nicked edge, a tiny inked cross nestling at its corner), the delicate order, the unique balance of the game would also begin to totter, to crumble, to disintegrate. The fine calibrations would sway as if they were a house, and not a game, of cards. The intricate order would have mutated, been changed in a manner at once infinitesimal and immense. Such a corruption of order would call everything everyone knew, had ever known, or would ever know into question: everything would still be connected to everything else, but nothing would mean anything.

The game was not a game of cards, much less a game of money: It was a game of life, played with cards. Everything had its sequence, everything had its order, no matter how random or unpredictable it should seem.

Whether the Galician was aware of this or not, no one knew. He merely sat, his cooling tea before him, unconcerned about the commotion his query had caused. And then he made another.

"What," he asked, "lies on the other side of the river?" The crowd looked at each other, blank faced. No one knew what was on the other side of the river. No one had thought to ask what lay on the other side of the river, over the bridge, on that far muddy or frosty bank.

"Bears," said someone, and there was a murmur of agreement, though all were in truth unsure. The story of the bears was dimly remembered, spurious at best. There was no lingering menace, no ancestral curse that lay over the far bank; it was simply that no one had the slightest interest.

"There is a map," Karm said to him, "in the Cartographer's shop. It shows the whole town, life-sized. Perhaps it also shows what lies over the other bank." No one knew because no one had consulted the map for many years, one said. It was no longer reliable, said another. In tatters, said a third.

By now the pack had been inspected and found to be in valid playing condition, and the tea, almost forgotten about, was judged cool enough.

The Marquis lifted his glass.

"One for salt!" he cried, and the crowd echoed him.

"One for salt!"

"One for iron!" he cried, and the crowd echoed him.

"One for iron!"

"One for blood!"

"One for blood!"

"... and one for the devil!"

(This last line was the Marquis's own addition to the rhyme that had opened the game ever since anyone could remember. It was not universally liked, some feeling it overly macabre, but the Marquis felt it gave his game a flourish, a distinction not seen among previous generations of players.)

The game could begin.

In truth, the game had already begun. The game had begun a long time ago, and once it had started, the game was always in progress. One story recounted the tale of a player who had died at table and carried on regardless. (Quite how the deceased player carried on is never told. It is perhaps more probable that it was his companions who carried on regardless.)

"A true champion," said Ada, whenever this story was told.

"A true hero," replied Eva, whenever she heard the story.

"To die doing what one loves doing most in this life, surely, is no death at all," said the Marquis, after he had told the story.

The game was being played whether the Marquis was at table or not. The game was being played even on the far side of the river. The game had always been played, and always would be.

The Marquis laid a card on the table: French suit, the Ace of Hearts. A simple, honest start, the crowd agreed. The classic opener for when a guest was playing, a show of welcome, of hospitality.

The Galician nodded but, before responding with a card of his own, made a further request.

"I would like the decks to be riffled and reshuffled."

Once again, the crowd grumbled and murmured, moaned and burbled. The request was licit, surely, this was known, but to certain players—whether onlookers or active participants—it implied not only a certain degree of bad faith, but something more.

Though the rules of the game were Daedalian, its method of play was simple. A number of strategies or gambits could be put into effect at any given point in the play by any player or group of players, much as in a game of chess. Over the years, such strategies had earned names: the Shepherd's Loss, the Sicilian Blade, the Swiss Entry, the Blacksmith's Lament, the Russian Linesman, the Dancing Horse, the Lame Swan, the Bottle of Smoke, the Tattooist's Daughter, the Drinker of Jasmine Tea, the Levantine Merchant, the Hungarian Dog's Back Leg.

The Galician's curious and unexpected questions had led the Marquis to a particular suspicion.

"I take it, Sir," said the Marquis, "that you intend to play the Blind Accordionist."

The Marquis knew, as Ada and Eva knew, as many of the assembled murmuring crowd knew, that the Blind Accordionist was one of the most controversial moves that could be made. The Blind Accordionist had never been played before; the Blind Accordionist had only ever been mentioned in hushed tones, spoken of behind closed doors, with nods of heads and grave faces and the low voices of men sitting in the quiet back room of the Golden Lion. The Blind Accordionist, it was said, would reorder everything, reconfigure the way in which the game was to be played.

And yet, the Marquis knew more than this.

"The Blind Accordionist," he whispered to Eva and Ada, "cannot ever be played."

"Why ever not?" asked Ada, or Eva.

"The Blind Accordionist," said the Marquis with gravity, "is the move that will end the game."

The game could not end.

Much as no one really knew how the game had begun, it was known that the game could not end. The game had always been, and would always be. The game could not end because the game could not ever be won or lost, because the game was life itself.

At this point, their options were limited. They could play a Bookbinder's Reel, or the Dandelion Clock; they could invoke the Drohobych Variant; they could use extra-ludic strategies (as far as anything could ever be outside of the game): having a telegram delivered to the Galician calling him home on urgent business, shouting "fire!," actually starting a fire. Other, darker, suggestions were made before being almost instantly dismissed.

There come times in every game, or every life, when chaos seems to be the constituent element. There are, if one is fortunate enough to know them, certain people for whom this is a moment not only of opportunity, but of meaning. Ada and Eva were two such people.

"Ada?" said Eva.

"Eva?" said Ada.

As if by clockwork, as if they had waited for this moment, as if this had all been planned and prepared, Ada and Eva moved in.

No subterfuge nor sleight of hand would be necessary. All that was needed was a reinterpretation of everything. A slight changing of the borders or the boundaries that would make everything—although completely different—stay exactly the same.

"The Galician," said Eva, "is simply a man in the wrong place."

"Or rather," corrected Ada, "we should say that there is no wrong place."

"Indeed," said Eva. "Location is all relative."

"Like time," said Ada.

"We simply need to reinterpret."

"To see from a different perspective."

"Are you suggesting," asked the Marquis, "that we change the rules?"

"The rules are always being changed," said Ada.

"There are no rules—that is the rule," said Eva. "There are no *things.*"

"Only events," said Ada.

"It is up to us to make a sequence of them."

"To give them pattern."

"Order."

"Form."

"Nothing can end," said Ada.

"Only change," said Eva.

The Galician looked at Eva, then at Ada, then at Ada, then at Eva. The cards were reshuffled. The Galician held his pack.

"Go ahead," said Ada.

"You may," said Eva.

It is said that the Galician then played a card, or cards, though no one who was there that night agrees on which or how many cards were placed on the table, or indeed if even any were at all. It is said that a wind came and blew all the cards away, that everyone was too drunk on pear brandy, and that the whole tale is a mere fiction, that Klug's dog spoke but that everyone was too busy worrying about everything else to actually listen to what, if anything, the hound had to say.

The only things that were certain is that the Galician left for Odessa, the Marquis continued to drink, and Ada and Eva even joined him, and everyone, everywhere, continued to be part of the game, because the game could not be stopped, because everyone was part of the game; even those who lay in the cemetery or continued to walk the streets of the town with no bodily form, memories only, they too played the game, because everybody is playing the game, even—yes, at this very moment, as you read this page—you.

PILGRIM
SOULS
— ♦ ♠ ♥ ♣ —

ON THE DAY they finished moving the cemetery, Alma Brik went to ten funerals. After eighty-eight years, the full strangeness of this world was nothing new to her, but ten funerals in a day was pushing it, especially as they were funerals for people for whom she had already attended funerals. She should go again, she told herself, if only to show the dead they had not been reforgotten.

It was late February, and the pear trees were already in bloom. Too soon, Alma knew, but the weather was warmer up here on this side of the valley. That wasn't the only strange thing, though, noted Alma: apples were growing on their boughs.

She thought of Doctor Albert, her neighbour, who used to tell her his outlandish dreams, even though she begged him not to and covered her ears when he spoke. Ten funerals in one day and apples growing on pear trees would have been dreams too strange even for Doctor Albert, she thought. He had stopped dreaming now, though. He hadn't had a single dream, he told her, since they moved the village.

The early evening light fell at an angle now unfamiliar to her. The shadows she had used to guide herself home had shifted, and she could no longer be sure she wouldn't end up lost. The snow had mostly cleared; what remained banked up into small rifts around the edges of the square. It looked more like ash, she thought.

Alma was pleased the oak had come with them. Ten strong men had uprooted the tree and heaved it onto a cart, which strained up the hillside, then replanted it in the new square. Some branches had been lost during the journey, so it no longer had quite the same shape, even though it was the same tree, in the same square, in the same village, only now in a different place. They moved the fountain, too, but not its source, so now the fountain ran dry.

When they opened the new village, the mayor had a ribbon put around the oak that he then cut, ceremonially, declaring the new village open. Everybody looked at one another and wondered what they should do now that their village, where they had lived for most of their lives, was officially open. Shortly after, as they went home, they were thinking of the mayor cutting the ribbon, and of the river drowning what remained of their original homes. They thought of their old walls collapsing under the weight of the water coursing onward, devouring everything until it hit the wall of the new dam at the bottom of the valley. Had she so wished, Alma could have stood in the cemetery and watched the water plough its path, filling the now-empty graves below. But she had not wished such a thing, and had instead sat herself in the new main square by the new old oak, uncertain as to what direction her new old home lay in.

She had continued to sit there, with many passersby not thinking it strange that the old woman should spend her days so.

When Lev returned to the village, twenty years after having left, he didn't even notice the woman sitting by the side of the square. He would already have regarded her as old back then, but Alma watched him come back, and remembered. Scarcely a boy he'd been when he left. There was much Lev did not notice. He did not notice, for example, the very fact that the village had moved.

Each brick, each stone, each tree, and each scrubby bush had been carried up the hillside and put back, both new and ancient. Exactly as it had been, they'd been promised, only *better*, they said: the new village would no longer be the worn-out old place it had been, the place the young ones left for the attractions of the city or other countries entirely. The new village would be brighter, more spacious, healthier. The new village would be closer to the new factories offering new jobs for the new people. The old village suffered from damp, they said, and it was true: its old walls ached to the point of collapse, worms ate its wooden beams, its old white paint was stained by eternal mildew. The new village was heated, hermetic, insulated. There was no space in the old houses, they said, they're too small for modern families. Nobody should have to go to a well for water nowadays, they said, no one should have to urinate in a field. So they built the new houses a little bigger than the old ones, a few feet more space for the floors, the ceilings a few hands higher. All the new houses were given a tiny plot to grow vegetables, run chickens, or tether a goat.

No one had told Lila any of this, but her aunt had given her the name of a village and a photograph of a rich man giving money to a blind beggar playing the accordion, and even though there was no map, she decided to make her way back to the place she had been born.

Alma remembered how the valley had suffered from gloom, damp, flies. In the winter, a clammy cold grew like mould on their bones. They forgot what warmth meant. In the summer, the heat slid down the hillside like butter and coagulated in the village. They forgot what cold meant. But now, up on the shoulder of the hill that leaned into the valley, it was healthier, they said, protected from strong winds but open to salutary breezes, warm in the winter and cool in the summer. It was lighter, it was drier, there was no fear of flooding. Their fingers, toes, and window frames wouldn't freeze in the winter and rot in the autumn; their plants wouldn't die of heatstroke in the barren August.

Leon had a map, but it still stank of all the damp and rot, all the foul air and gloom. His father had drawn it for him, and his father had not been to the village for twenty years. His father, a man to whom words were strange things, had read no newspaper and took no heed of gossip. Leon hadn't even heard of the place until a week ago and lacked the basic skills needed to read a map, but this mattered little to him. He had asked where the village was, people had pointed, he had arrived.

Alma watched them all pass, Lev, Lila and Leon, but knew she could not help them. Nothing was as it had been. Mirrors had stopped reflecting her directly, and showed only oblique angles of the room she stood in. Her own face was unrecognisable. Clocks carried on ticking, but their hands cast no shadow. In the yard of her new old house, time itself had slowed to the speed of thick honey sliding from a spoon.

Little surprise Lev didn't realise the town had moved; he hardly remembered leaving. Then, twenty years ago, he had nothing in mind other than the journey ahead and had deliberately ignored what lay behind. Now, though, he remembered the square perfectly, with its oak tree and its fountain, places they'd played as children, then where they sat and schemed to escape as young lovers. As he wandered in search of the exact spot, he found other places he remembered: the school, the clump of trees where he'd first kissed his first love, the close behind the church where he'd asked her to marry him. He feared recognition, but the few people he saw took no notice of him, nor he of them. He wondered how much he had changed in twenty years. Some of the buildings seemed newer now than when he had left. At the bottom of the hill stood a lake that he didn't remember, thinking of it only that the millpond had perhaps grown. He had swum in it, he remembered, his feet touching the bottom.

The whole village, strangely, looked bigger now.

Lila hoped for clues carved in trees and on benches, but found nothing. She didn't even know her father's first name. She hoped to talk to men in the café and women in the shops but didn't dare enter the dark café, and the shop girls looked at her picture of the blind man with the accordion as if it were nothing but a blank sheet of paper. Try the cemetery, they said. Lila hoped not to find her family name on a headstone. She met a man who smiled and told her he had begun to dream again, because how else could he be seeing a girl he'd known fifty years ago, unchanged?

Leon wasn't surprised to find his map made little sense. The lines on the paper only approximated the lines made by the streets. The small pond was a significant lake, far below. A fat tree and a fountain stood in the main square, though the tree was clearly dying and the fountain didn't work. He would never find the man he'd been sent to find, he thought. This village, with its walls bereft of the scratches and marks and signs that time makes, its silence as deep as the lake below, and its lost populace shuffling around in search of yesterday, was no place the man who had stolen his father's fortune would come to hide. There were no riches here.

Alma sat in the cemetery and listened. On quiet days—and all the days were quiet now—she could hear voices, and she wondered if she were hearing the dreams Doctor Albert no longer dreamt. Some days, when the breeze drew up from the valley below, she could hear the church bells ringing under the water, even though the bells hung in the church behind her now and were always silent. She wondered what had happened to the ghosts. Had they moved with the village, or got lost on the way, or were they still there, wandering around under the water?

As Lev searched, he remembered things he'd never noticed before: the angle of the climbing sun, the distant sound of water, the colour of the railings around the school, the smell of milk. He sat on the low wall behind the mill and remembered that moment when their shadows had stretched out together, becoming one in the distance. He stayed there until it grew dark, watching his single shadow lengthen and lose distinction until it vanished entirely, swallowed by the surrounding dark. And then he started to dig. This, he was sure, this was the place. This was the last place he'd seen her, and the place where he'd buried what he kept of her memory, the thing he'd come back to find.

In the cemetery, Lila saw freshly tilled earth and did not dare read names inscribed on wooden crosses. She showed her picture to an old woman there, but thought the woman blind, as she seemed to see nothing and be very lost. *May I guide you home?* Lila asked, and the old woman smiled and nodded, and took her arm.

Leon thought the problem with his map was one of scale: the streets here weren't as narrow as the lines on his paper. There was light here, and none of the heavily crosshatched darkness. Perhaps his father had never visited this place, his thieving uncle much less. He sat on the bench in the square and began to realise that he had been sent on a wild errand.

Alma thought for a moment that the kind young woman in the cemetery was a ghost, then realised, as she took her warm and fleshly arm, that she wasn't, and she realised then that there were no ghosts, that the ghosts hadn't come with them to the new village.

Leon wondered if he had got the wrong place altogether, and if his uncle had made off with the family fortune in the shape of a gold ring and set up in another village, the shadow-self of this one, somewhere on the other side of the valley. He was in the wrong place, it was certain, but it was better than the place he had been, the place to which he couldn't return empty-handed anyhow. It was quiet here, and sunny. There were no ghosts here, he thought, and he liked that. A man could live in this place, he thought, even without the benefit of stolen riches. Yes, he thought, I'll stay here.

As she walked the old woman through the streets, Lila looked out for the kind of men who might have helped beggars, but she saw none, and wondered if her father had not been the rich man giving money, but the other man in the picture. Her journey to find him would be long yet, she thought, and difficult. But was she never to succeed, would that be so bad?

Lev filled in the hole after having spent a fruitless hour sifting through the dry dirt to find what he had buried twenty years earlier. He thought about going to the cemetery to see if her name were there, but was scared to go at night. He dug under the railings where he'd first met her, then by the fountain where they'd played, by the trees where they'd kissed and the place where he had proposed, but found nothing.

As the sun came up, he left the village and walked down to the edge of the lake. Jug handles, bottle tops, and chair legs poked out of its muddy bank, and he wondered where they had all come from. He rubbed his eyes with the heels of his hands to take away his tiredness and smelled perfume. A plant he had brushed against, perhaps, or even the calm green lake water, but no, this was a human smell, even though he had shaken no one's hand, touched no one, not even spoken to anyone. The smell brought back a memory, nothing he could visualise or even put into words, but with a disturbing clarity. This was what he had been looking for: not an object, but the memory itself.

He turned to leave and a glint in the mud caught his eye. He bent down, then picked up and polished a gold ring, the very one he had offered to her, the one he had buried when she had refused, swearing to come back for it only when he was in love again. Only when he remembered was he free to forget.

As Alma let the young woman guide her, she could smell smoke, and it made her think of baking bread. She couldn't remember the last time it had rained, and in times of drought, she knew, fire blazed on the hills around them. Once by water, once by fire, she thought, but it mattered little. She was nearly home now.

AN INCIDENT ON THE TRAIN TO LVOV

———— ♦ ♠ ♥ ♣ ————

A POSTER ON the wall beside the ticket office promised glorious holidays in N—. The first gentleman said he had never been to N—, but that the poster had quite enticed him; the second man said that he had been to N— and that it was really quite an awful place. The first woman said she had never heard of N—, while the second woman said only that she knew the work of the artist who had done the picture of the famous funicular railway in N— and had always found his work to be rather second rate.

"Do you take an interest in art, Miss?" asked the first man to the second woman, and the second woman replied that she did, but only of the modern kind.

When the train (a huge black locomotive, billowing steam and spitting coals, an infernal spark from which burned a hole clean through the second gentleman's Gladstone bag) arrived, the four found themselves seated in the same compartment.

"I wondered, Sir," said the first man to the second, "on seeing your bag, if you were in the same profession as I?" The second man replied merely that he doubted it, as he was not in much of a profession at all.

"The bag was given to me some time ago," he said. "I find it useful for travelling, and little more." This was why the hole so recently burned into it, he explained, left him reasonably untroubled. "It is no great mischief."

The first woman, unused to the professional significance of travelling bags, asked the first man what his profession was.

"I am a physician, Ma'am, on my way to visit a complex patient." The man awaited further inquiries as to the specific nature of his patient's complexity, but when none came, he decided to continue the conversation. "And you, Ma'am, may I ask where you are bound?"

"I am visiting my brother," she said. "He is a writer, and he is dangerously ill."

The second woman suggested that the two people—the physician's complex patient and the first woman's ailing brother— might be one and the same person, but the Doctor and the woman both laughed at the suggestion without probing it further, most probably for fear that it should turn out to be true.

The two women could have been sisters. They shared the same nose, the tip of which upturned like the eastern end of Lake Balaton. In other ways, however, they differed: the first had hair that may once have been red, while the second (younger) woman had hair the colour of a particularly lustrous horse chestnut. She did not say why she was travelling.

The two men could not have been brothers. As unlike each other in temperament as in looks, the Doctor—who sported an unfashionable top hat that caused his head to overheat—was phlegmatic, cordial, convivial, and slightly conceited, while the younger man wore a scowl and a black suit grown shiny from overuse and undercleaning.

(There was, in truth, a fifth person in the compartment, but that was myself, and I pretended to sleep for much of what followed, so I shall make no further mention of him.)

The train hauled out of the station and the conductor passed along the corridor, apparently in some haste, as he did not ask to see tickets, nor even turn to face the passengers in the compartment. Everyone, however, noted his smart, well-pressed uniform, the bright green band around his cap, and the thick gleaming hair protruding from it.

"How young the Conductor is," remarked the first woman, and all the others concurred.

The Doctor produced a pack of cards.

"The journey is long," he said. "Shall we pass the time with a game?"

"I once heard a story," began the second man, "about a group of people on a train who played a game of cards. The game went on for days after the train became blocked in a huge snowdrift."

"Let us hope the same thing does not happen to us!" said the older woman.

"The game of cards, or the snowdrift?" responded the younger. It was agreed that the second option was improbable. It was late spring by now; Easter had passed, and with it even the remote possibility of snow.

"How did the game end?" asked the Doctor.

"The train was set upon by a pack of bandits."

"Let us hope the same thing does not happen to us!" said the older woman.

"That is unlikely," said the man. "This took place in Russia."

It was agreed that Russia was a place filled with bandits and outlaws, and that their own journey would be safe.

The Doctor discreetly replaced the pack of cards in his breast pocket, consoling himself that there would certainly be a game waiting for him once he reached his destination.

The younger woman produced a small magazine from her travelling bag and began to read. The other occupants of the compartment all politely strained their necks in order to discern the title of the magazine, and—perhaps—deduce something more about the young woman from her choice of reading matter. The only thing they could see was the title of the publication, which was called *L'accordéoniste aveugle.*

"May I ask," asked the Doctor, "what you are reading?'

"A review of French poetry," replied the young woman.

"Of the modern kind?" asked the Doctor.

"Oh yes," said the woman. "Terribly modern, I'm afraid."

All fell into silence for a considerable time.

The train travelled. The Doctor hummed a tune. The younger man gazed out of the window. The younger woman's eyes went in and out of focus, the older woman watched her. The train travelled through the endless unspooling countryside. The Doctor hummed his tune more loudly before breaking into speech.

"Yes," he said. "A train compartment really is the most perfect place for the telling of stories." None of the other passengers disagreed or agreed with him. "I was once on a train," he continued, oblivious to his travelling companions' lack of assent or dissent, "and I overheard a story being told. I tried to listen in, but realised that the teller of the tale wasn't telling the truth, and moreover, the listener was hearing something else entirely."

The younger woman had, at this point, her curiosity piqued.

"What was this story?" she asked.

"It's rather difficult to say," replied the Doctor. "One person was speaking Russian, the other German. Neither of those are languages I know."

They all fell into silence again, and the older woman fell asleep. Once asleep, she began to dream, and this is what she dreamt: She was in her childhood home, moving slowly through its long corridors. The house was completely empty, and felt strangely vacant to her. She went into the living room and stood before the fireplace. All the furniture had been removed, and a large mirror hung on the wall, reflecting nothing at all. (Later, when she recalled the dream, she would wonder if it were not a mirror, but perhaps a painting that somehow managed to depict a total absence.) No fire burned, but she looked at the large clock on the mantelpiece whose hands sat at a quarter to twelve (or perhaps, she recalled later, nine o'clock). Then a train came roaring out of the fireplace.

The others agreed that it was a most curious dream when the woman, on waking, told them where she had been.

"One of the earliest memories I have," said the younger woman, "is very like a dream, and indeed has become so confused in my mind over the years that I am now not at all sure that it wasn't, in fact, a dream." She continued, "I had a sister, once. Strange as it may seem, I never knew if we were sisters or twins— we were so close in age, and our mother made us wear dresses that were identical but for their slightly different colours. We lived very close to a large forest, and when it grew dark we would sometimes go out exploring. One night, we found a station in the forest. It had only three tracks and a small white ticket office, and although there were no other people there, two locomotives were steaming and ready to leave. We chose one, and got on. We travelled together for many years, across many places, until one day, when we were twenty, my sister got off the train and never came back. I have been looking for her ever since."

At this point the train ground to a halt in one of those very small country stations, as if to remind them that they were not dreaming. There was some commotion farther down the train, a man not knowing if it was his stop or not, but the train halted for a few minutes only and they were soon on their way again, the train heaving itself back into its heavy, ceaseless motion.

"I once heard a similar story," said the Doctor. "A man got off a train and stayed forever. His head was turned, you see, by a young woman he saw on the platform. He jumped out and tried to follow her, but then, I believe, lost her in the crowd. The train left without him, but it seemed to have been of little consequence, for I hear he simply decided to stay in the town, and spent the rest of his life there."

"That is quite a coincidence," said the younger man, "as very much the same thing happened to me. No woman turned my head, though, as I was travelling with my companion, with whom I was very happy. I cannot now remember quite why I disembarked at a lonely station—I was hungry, perhaps, or in search of something to read, and there was neither dining car nor library on board. As I say, I cannot remember; it matters little. I got off, and for a moment, I remember the entire world stopping. I wondered how it would be to simply stay there, to never move again, to become a different person, and start a new life in this remote place of which I knew nothing, and where no one knew me. When I came out of the reverie, I found the train had departed. The next train didn't arrive until a day later, but a porter told me he could take me as far as the next station in his trap. If the roads were good and the weather stayed clement, he said, we may be able to get there before the train arrived. The roads were good and the weather clement, and we arrived at the station to see the train that I had so recently vacated just heaving into view. I leapt aboard as soon as I could and ran along the corridor to find my companion. When I reached the compartment where we had been sitting, however, I found it vacant. She had gone. I asked the conductor, the other passengers, but no one had seen her. I have travelled looking for her ever since. I am doing so at this very moment."

"For me," said the older woman, "it is different. I always have the feeling that someone is following me."

At this point the train passed over a deep ravine, the sound of the engine momentarily falling away beneath them as steeply and quickly as the land. The Doctor told everyone that, fifteen years previously, a train had derailed while crossing this bridge, and all the passengers had died, plunging into the river far below.

"The most terrible thing," he continued, "was that among them was a party of schoolchildren, on their way to visit the waterfalls." Travelling by train, they all agreed, could sometimes be a most dangerous method of transportation.

To lighten the mood, they all spoke of how magnificent it would be when they arrived. The station, they told each other, was known to be a miracle worked by artists, architects, and engineers, a cathedral to house the railway gods, a frozen dance of delicate glass and iron tracery, a wonder for the modern world.

"I know of a person," said the younger woman, "who took up residence in a railway station."

"That seems to me," said the younger man, "a fine solution."

The conductor came back asking for their tickets. Now he was turned toward them, his face—imagined as being smooth, handsome, and unblemished—was revealed as gnarled and haggard, with deep frown lines and purple sags below the eyes. His journey to the far end of the train had aged him, it seemed. Everyone in the compartment felt as though they had already spent days on this train, yet were also aware that outside, it was possible that only a few minutes had passed.

"There is a train," said the Doctor, "that crosses the great plains of South America, or Upper Canada, possibly, that is so long that the conductor has a map, but even he has never visited its far end, or its beginning. It takes years, even at great velocity, to travel from its departure to its destination." The others all fell silent, imagining such a thing, which disturbed them all greatly.

At that point, the train disappeared into a tunnel and everything went dark, and for a moment none of them were sure if they had been telling different stories, or different parts of the same story.

PETER, WHO THOUGHT HE WAS A BEAR

♦ ♠ ♥ ♣

WHEN HIS WIFE announced she was leaving him for the fat man who tended the bar at the inn on the square, Peter began to believe he was a bear. He performed a few circuits of their tiny kitchen, heavy trudging steps and hunched shoulders, his wife still looking on, bemused, then slightly horrified.

There is no more of me, thought Peter as his wife took what she wanted. I am a bear now.

Here begins the story of Peter the bear.

Peter let his hair and his beard grow. He did not wash frequently, nor change his clothes. He took to drinking in the other tavern, the one on the far edge of town, and had to take the long way there, the unpaved path that curved around the remoter houses and just touched the woods, then the same one to come home again, late at night, alone and slightly drunk. Though he could not see them, he knew other bears were there, along the road, hiding just behind the bushes or in the trees, waiting for him.

At first he was scared, but later, as he began to make the journey more frequently, he realised the bears were everywhere, in the long grass, the backyards, the shadows, and even behind the walls, and they meant him no harm.

Let us tell the story of Peter who thought he was a bear.

Peter heard that his wife had moved in with the fat man, her new home a small room above the bar. One day, he saw her near the market, carrying a bag full of onions, and she turned, but when she turned she did not see Peter but waved to the fat man who was coming toward her, across the square. The fat man was hairy, and it was known that he smelled bad, but he was not like a bear. Peter heard his wife and the fat man laughing, and he did not know if they had seen him or not.

Even though the winter had fully passed now, and spring was beginning to twitch, Peter continued to wear his big coat, and continued to let his beard grow. He did not sleep in his bed but sat at the table that they had once shared, and pulled a rug over his lap, and slept there. He threw away his razor.

Let us wonder, let us marvel, at how like a real bear Peter is. His hair, his skin, his peculiar gait.

After Easter, the Circus came. There would be bears, Peter knew. The Circus pitched on the far edge of town, on the empty field Peter passed on his way to drink, the place where he had thought there were bears, in the trees, the bushes. I was right, thought Peter. There were bears, but they have been waiting for the Circus, not for me.

The Circus, the Circus, the Circus has come!

When the Circus opened, Peter did not go, as he did not wish to be entertained by clowns, enchanted by acrobats, or scared by lions. He did not wish to see his wife there with the fat man, being entertained, or enchanted, or scared. Peter went to the Circus, but he stayed outside. He wanted to talk to the bears.

But the bears did not want to talk to Peter. They stood in small sad circles, not even speaking to each other. The bears smelled bad, thought Peter, but not in the same way the fat man who tended the bar smelled bad. The bears smelled of oil and sadness.

On the last night of the Circus it rained heavily, and Peter waited by the main entrance of the tent. Inside it was nearly empty, and, after the clowns had entertained, the acrobats had enchanted, and the lions had scared, the bears began to dance, and Peter made use of the dark to slip inside. He sat on a wooden bench as close to the back as he could. There were few people in the Circus, and the rain beat down on its waxed canvas and oil-cloth covers. The bears moved in time with the sound of the rain and a handheld drum. A single-stringed violin scratched a slow tune into the silence.

Can we hear, can we? The bear music that Peter hears?

Peter's friends began to avoid him. They did not like his method of eating, his silence, or surliness. His bearness. Peter carried on drinking in the tavern on the far edge of the town, where the few friends he had left did not join him. Sometimes, when he drank, Peter wished he could have become a wolf, or an eagle, or even a snake, perhaps. Something faster, smoother, with sharper teeth and sleeker skin. Other times, he wished he could have believed himself a worm, or a beetle, or something more fitting to his current state of being. But bear he had been given; bear it would be.

One night of lonely drunkenness, Peter walked home with a bottle in his hand. He threw the bottle at a wall, but the bottle did not break with a satisfying crash and a splatter of liquor; it merely bounced off the wall and rolled along the path. He picked it up and again tried to break it, but it would not break. Were I a bear, thought Peter, I could shatter this glass with my rage. But then he remembered the Circus bears, and they had been gentle, shy creatures, filled only with sadness and furtiveness, never anger.

Let us wonder at how little like a bear Peter is.

Every night he sat alone in the bar, even when the place was full. Some nights he looked only at the table before him, his hands that lay on it, or the glass that held his beer; other nights he watched drinkers talking and laughing amongst themselves.

On Saturdays, the tavern was always full, and there was warmth and music, smoking and dancing. Peter did not want to dance, or if he did, to dance only the way he had seen the bears at the Circus dance.

If only everyone could be as sad as I am, he thought. If only everyone could be a bear.

He approached a man he had once known and told him all about being a bear, but the man refused to listen, so Peter tried talking to a woman, who looked at him with pity before she walked away.

No, not everyone, Peter, not everyone can be a bear.

Peter missed the bears, even though they had not been friendly, and he waited anxiously for the Circus to return, even though he knew it would not be for another year. He decided to go into the woods and join them.

He found a small clearing, lay a tarpaulin on the ground, and slung his old overcoat across two branches. The rain came in a little, but he did not mind. He built himself a fire, which smoked a lot because the wood was damp.

No bears came to visit him, nor could he find any.

After a few days, he returned to his empty house, cold and hungry and developing a serious chill. The bears, he thought, did not want his company.

Let us, let us not, weep for Peter.

Peter thought about how he looked now, and how he walked, and how he acted, and then he thought about his life before. He thought that he had, perhaps, always been a bit bear, and sometimes did not wonder that his wife had left him.

For a while, Peter tried not to be so bear. He stood up full straight when he walked, trying not to slouch. He waved at anyone who should pass his house and look in the window. He washed regularly. He shaved all the hair off his body, for fear of how ursine he had become.

Peter heard that his wife had left the fat man, too, and that the fat man had drunk a bottle of rat poison. He felt no pity, only realised that perhaps his wife had gotten what she wanted.

Within a month, after no one had returned his friendly wave, the hair had grown back again, and his slouch fell back into place.

Peter, Peter—will this music never stop? How will our tale be told?

After a year in which each day passed the same, the Circus returned. This time, Peter was prepared. He waited until night, then walked past the tent, past the carts and caravans where the Circus people snored, as far as the edge of the field where the bears slept in their cages. They growled when he poked them with his stick, but only one of them woke. The bear sat up and looked at Peter slowly.

"No," said the bear, "you are not a bear, this will pass." The bear wiped at his face with a heavy paw. "Being a bear," it continued, "is far worse than what you are suffering."

Later that night, or perhaps it was another night, Peter watched the bears do their dance again. They all arose and unlocked their cages and stood in a careful circle at the edge of the field, beyond where the Circus tent was pitched, and far from where they could be seen. Other bears, the bears from the woods, came to join their fellow bears, taking their place in the circle. They took a step forward, a step back, one to the left, one to the right. Each bear in turn raised their left paw, then their right. Each bear in turn stepped into the middle of the circle and did a slow pirouette, then returned to the circle. There was no music, but Peter could hear it anyway, played on a violin with a broken string, a sealskin drum, and a wheezing accordion by musicians who were all blind.

Peter wondered how many of the bears from the Circus or from the woods had once been men or women like him, who had been happy and lived in the town with husbands or wives or children, and had had jobs about which they complained, and friends with whom they could drink and smoke and talk of inconsequential things. He thought he should go into the woods again, or wait another year for the Circus and find a bear and offer to change places with them.

Oh, Peter, the bears are not for you, whatever you may think!

When spring came again and the cold held back, then early summer with its clearer skies and softer rain, Peter's hands stopped being so heavy, so much like shovel blades or the heads of lump hammers, and his cramped fingers creaked and stretched as he began to write a letter. *It was the sadness,* he wrote, *it was the sadness that was all too much.*

He drafted the letter many times, and each time replaced it at the back of the drawer where he kept things he wanted to forget, and he thought he could, perhaps, take it to the bears who were still out there, waiting, ready to welcome him whenever he wanted.

AT THE GALLERY
OF NATIONAL ART

───────── ♦ ♠ ♥ ♣ ─────────

I AM A WARDER at the Gallery of National Art, and I pass each day in silence. I sit in a narrow chair and watch the pictures on the walls, the people who wander by, and the motes of dust in the thick air. I am a Warder at the Gallery of National Art, and my work is precious to me: as a Warder, I protect the art of my nation from thieves and cast light on it for the curious. Though my work may seem simple, depth often passes unseen: I am both guard and guide.

The guiding is not so common. On occasion I am called on to direct those looking for a specific piece of National Art, though rarely am I asked questions about it. Although I say my work is precious to me, I do not love my job. I am a Warder, after all: my job is to sit, and guard, and guide, and this I do.

The guarding is constant, but in truth makes me fearful. Even in our small country, there have been stories of clever, scheming thieves who would wish to deprive our nation, and keep the

National Art for their private pleasures. I worry about violent confrontation, much as I know the possibility of such confrontation to be slim. Those who desire to steal are far more likely to enter the Gallery of National Art by night when I am at home and sleeping in my bed. And yet I am on constant watch for those who make repeated visits and display more interest in skylights than the National Art itself. There have, in truth, been no thefts at the Gallery of National Art in the time I have been a Warder here. If you are seeking stories of dangerous criminals foiled with aplomb and derring-do, I apologise, for I have none.

Among my serried days of dust and silence, few moments stand out. While I have no love for my job, nor do I hold any hate, and sometimes I am startled into feeling: this morning, for example, a young girl came to me and asked me a question at which I marvelled. I have been thinking on the answer to her question for some considerable time now, and still I have not found it.

Yet there are other days when I am filled with the void. In this respect, I believe I am much like the rest of humanity. I try not to think of such days, and instead, as I sit on my narrow chair, I consider the times when I have had the opportunity to explain pieces of our National Art. Many visitors, especially those few who come from other countries, shuffle along in silence, their noses pushed firmly into a guidebook. One day, perhaps soon, there will be no further need for Warders at the Gallery of National Art; we shall be replaced by guidebooks, and I shall be made redundant, but this day has not yet come.

I say I am much like the rest of humanity, but in truth I do not know. Does much of humanity veer between wonder and the void? I do not know, because as a Warder at the Gallery of National Art, my work allows me little space for friends.

I prefer it if visitors ask why the pictures are organised so, or if a certain artist could be said to pertain to a specific school, or who the figure in a portrait is, or where the events shown in a particular painting took place. Sometimes they ask how they may widen their knowledge and understanding of the art of our nation. I even like it when they ask me if we have any Italian nativities, or Flemish interiors, or English sailing ships, and I patiently explain that no, we have none, because this is a gallery of National Art. These questions are posed less frequently now. Perhaps the guidebooks are more accurate and better annotated, or perhaps with the passing of time I have faded like the delicate cartoons we keep in Room 12.

Faded as I may be, I like to think it is my very presence that wards off thieves as they prowl the Gallery searching for potential trophies and unlocked windows.

As a Warder at the Gallery of National Art, I know the contents of each room perfectly, intimately. Ask me what the first picture on the left in Room 1 is, for example, and I would be able to tell you that it is a roughly put together genre painting of a group of topers and card sharps seated around a table in a country tavern. The final picture on the right in Room 52? A woman walking a narrow path away from a large, dilapidated house toward the woods that cover the rest of the canvas. It is late summer, early evening, the light perfectly evoked.

The third picture from the left on the main wall in Room 23 depicts a house whose brick façade is painted in a delicate duck-egg blue with a single lamp illuminating its door. I know this house well, because it is the house where I live. As I enter the gallery in the morning or leave at night, I often glimpse the painting and think of my home waiting for me. In winter, by the time I arrive home, the pool of light around the door has not expanded but intensified, while the rest of the house has vanished in gloom. At the same time, I believe the picture stays exactly as it is. I find my key and open the door and climb the three flights of stairs to the small flat where I live alone now, and I eat at my table before sleeping. My life is quiet, circumscribed. I am a Warder at the Gallery of National Art.

Although there have been no thefts on my watch, a man once attacked a work of our National Art. His eyes were set a little too close together, his hair was threadbare, and he wore a jacket with its buttons missing. He made several circuits of the gallery, and I noticed him because he was alone, and I always take special care to notice lone visitors, not because I believe them potential criminals, but because I find their singleness palpable. His forehead glistened, and, though alone, he spoke aloud. Each time he passed his voice grew, his words ever denser and less comprehensible. On his fourth circuit, he pushed his hand deep into the pocket of his jacket and pulled out a small hammer, the kind you would use to nail a picture tack into a wall, and he approached the large statue of King Ata that stood in the middle of the room, and he set about the statue with his hammer. A splinter flew from the King's kneecap, his toe was smashed, and his arm came off in but a few seconds. I shouted for help but none came, so I restrained the man myself. It was not difficult. His heart was not in it. He did not really want to kill God, as he later told the court. Perhaps he had wanted to kill his father. I do not know. I am not a Viennese doctor. I am a Warder at the Gallery of National Art.

Today is a good day, not only because of the question the girl asked, but also because I am working in the portraits room of the Gallery, sitting directly opposite a tiny picture the size of a small envelope, the type of envelope that would contain a handwritten invitation to a birthday party or a lightly perfumed love letter. The picture is of a young person who, I believe, looks exactly like me. Were I ever asked to name my favourite picture in the Gallery of National Art, I would choose this one. It is not a well-executed picture, the brushwork jagged and approximate and the paint laid too thickly, but even though I am now undoubtedly older than the anonymous figure in the picture, and although no one has ever pronounced on the likeness, I feel it a mirror into another version of myself.

Next to the portraits room is the gallery of trains. There have been no trains in our nation, and many wonder why there should be so many pictures of them. Some time ago, there was much talk of the coming of the trains, and a competition was held. Painters were asked to depict the trains they imagined for our nation. No winner was ever declared, and the railroad never came. I used to hope that the train would arrive in our country in my lifetime, but when I look at the hundreds of tiny paintings crammed into the gallery, and the four enormous ones, I think I shall be glad if I never see a real train. They seem monstrous to me, iron, steam, and fire, waiting to take me away.

Some days are so slow I count the bricks in the walls, or measure the size of the room using units I have only in my mind. It is surprising that no two rooms in the gallery are exactly the same size. One day I returned home to find that I would be living alone. My small flat is still the same but has a hole in it like the discoloured space that remains on the gallery wall when a picture has been removed.

Another painting I love, though I cannot explain why, is the strangest picture in the Gallery of National Art. Many visitors walk directly past this picture, thinking it merely a blank canvas. It hangs in the landscape rooms, though it is not quite a landscape: It is a picture of nothing, if that is possible. It shows an enormous plain, not quite desert nor quite tundra, endlessly unfolding. Though empty, it pulls with the gravity of an enormous planet. I do not understand its composition, it is no banal trickery of the eye, no geometric cleverness, but it works with perception in such a way as to seem infinite, though of course I know that cannot possibly be so. Once, the gallery completely empty, I stood so close to this picture that I feared the touch of my breath would damage its paint, and I let it envelop me. The picture ceased to become space, and became time. It is inexplicable and vast, and that is why I love it so. The ghosts who frequent the gallery sometimes crowd around this picture, perhaps because it reminds them of where they live.

I am a Warder at the Gallery of National Art, and in my job, every day is like a recurring dream: always the same, and always different.

Visitors from abroad sometimes come to me and say it should not be the "Gallery of National Art" but the "National Gallery of

Art," and I tell them as politely as I can that they are mistaken. This is not a national gallery, but it does house national art. This gallery is a home to art that displays our nation. They call me a guard, these visitors, or they call me a guide, and I say I am not a guard or a guide but it is my job to do both of these things because I am a Warder at the Gallery of National Art.

The ghosts are heavy today, whereas sometimes months pass without one visiting at all.

In winter, I eat soup and black bread, in summer yoghurt and nuts, and I keep despair tightly sealed in a jar hidden at the back of the top shelf of the cupboard I rarely use. When I think of sadness, I think of the delicate cartoons in darkened Room 12, covered with a heavy felt blanket.

The works in the Gallery of National Art are not grouped along lines of chronology or artistic movement, I sometimes have to tell visitors, but into landscapes, portraits, and histories. There are pictures of the natural beauties and wonders of our country; there are pictures of the important people in the development of our nation; and there are pictures of the Battle of the River Slem, the Signing of the Treaty of Vla, the building of Liberation Bridge, and the opening of the gallery itself.

Even though it is not my job as a Warder at the Gallery of National Art to decide such things, based on my long contemplations and my admittedly infrequent exchanges with visitors to the gallery, I have sometimes wondered if there may be better ways to organise the pictures. I think the works should be gathered into rooms for circular, rectangular, and triangular pictures, perhaps, or those made by left- or right-handed artists, or rooms containing true and false works. Works painted by day, and those by night. The differences are subtle, but essential.

There are questions that are never asked of me, and sometimes I am grateful for this fact. Were I asked, for example, I would be obliged to tell anyone who wanted to know that the small but intricate landscape that hangs in Room 13, next to the famous painting called *The Sea-Sprite*, is not in fact by the artist named on its label but is actually a forgery, painted by a less well-known but no less interesting artist. The story of the forgery is more interesting than the story of the real painting, which I now believe hangs in the bedroom of a man who cares very little for it, but it is perhaps a story best left untold.

Since the day the man with threadbare hair attacked the statue of King Ata, I have felt less safe in my job. It is only on days like today, when I am asked a question that illuminates me, that I still feel confident that my work is precious.

More than the pictures, the thing I love most about being a Warder at the Gallery of National Art is the silence. Even on the rare days the gallery is crowded, there is always a silence so deep it cannot be disturbed. Over time, the silence has grown so dense that not even noisy schoolchildren or gaggles of tourists can disturb it. The silence always has a further fold that can be entered, thick with dust, a lovely carpet that covers the days. Even whispers are muted by the gallery's silence, a silence so heavy it could slow time itself.

I am a Warder at the Gallery of National Art, and I am familiar with the Gallery's many ghosts. I have spent years watching them pass through the halls. There are the painters who still want to change their paintings. There are those who were lost here, or had nowhere else to go. One I do not know: a small child who wanders the galleries. Some are like us, but smaller, while others are shadowy, never quite in focus, as if moving too quickly or too slowly for us to perceive.

The ghosts in the gallery come and go frequently, some with more or less bodily form, others totally invisible, merely manifesting as a strong smell. There it is now: Roast bacon. Pipe smoke. Cough medicine.

Some days, an ache dulls the small of my back, or my legs begin to twitch and I have to stand and pace the room slowly. Though this is uncomfortable, I am content because I know then that, yes, I am alive, and, yes, I do exist. Though I see the ghosts, I am not yet one of their number.

Some pictures in the gallery baffle me, no matter how many days I pass watching them. One such picture shows two people standing on opposing sides of a river. It is maybe the River Slem, which runs through our country. They face each other and regard each other carefully, but without recognition. It may be a history picture, but the people are not famous. One is much older than the other. I feel it is connected to the picture that hangs opposite, though I do not know how. This shows two villages, identical, but for the fact one nestles into the shade of a deep valley, while the other stands up on the hill above. Both are deserted.

A fuzzy shape hovers beside another picture in this room, a dark portrait of a troubled, bear-like man, and I am the only one able to see it. I think it another ghost, and believe it to be the picture's painter, forever stuck on a pentimento he will never be able to make. I see the ghosts of the future, too, sometimes: the ones who have not happened yet, but will.

Another picture I do not understand is a still life showing a table piled with lacemakers' bobbins. There are so many of them, so intricate. The detail, the reels of thread untangling and retangling. It is so different to another baffling picture, the one that is called "The Blind Accordionist." The picture has no official name, and no one knows why it is nicknamed so, as it shows nothing but an empty doorway leading into an interior space that is scarcely visible.

I had a surprise today: a man I recognised came into the gallery. This is not so surprising in itself, as I recognise many of our frequent visitors, but this man is not a frequent visitor. The reason I know this man is other. This man, older now, his unshaven chin hanging from his shrunken face and a felt cap on his head, is the man who forged the landscape painting in Room 13 and was complicit in consigning the original to the former lover of the man in whose bedroom it now hangs. I took the excuse of the regular break I am permitted to follow him as far as the room where his handiwork is displayed. He stood for a good while before the picture, grinning and muttering to himself, taking pleasure in his craft and, quite possibly, in his deception. I do not consider him a bad man, but wish he had put his talent to better use. I wonder about the man who tried to destroy the statue. He has never returned. I do not know what happened to him.

I was once asked if I had ever wanted to do anything else in my life, and I could not reply, because this is all I have ever

done. I am not unsatisfied with my life. I think about my favourite picture in the gallery, the portrait who looks like me.
I wonder if this was a self-portrait, and if the artist looked like
me. I have never wanted to paint. I like looking. I am a Warder
at the Gallery of National Art.

Only one picture in the Gallery of National Art scares me. It
shows three forest wolves walking in a circle, each closely pursu-
ing the other. One of them looks out at me. They have eaten of the
darkness, these wolves, and they know me. Taken in time, they
are trapped in the picture, and one day I fear they will escape.

In our history section, we have a picture of King Ata talking to
a commoner. The king is in disguise, and the commoner is blind.
Everyone knows the story, but it is not so familiar to foreign
guests, who often walk past the picture. I like to wonder if one of
them is a king in disguise, or that I might be a king, ready to give
a revelation to a passerby, to condemn them to death, or hand
them my crown. I think that I am not a Warder at the Gallery
of National Art, but that I am every one of the people who has
passed, is passing, or will pass through its halls.

Today has been as similar and as different as any day, but it
has been one of the better ones. This evening as I was preparing
to leave, an old woman came into the gallery and told me how she
had held my hand, many years ago, and asked me a question that
dazzled me, and to which I could not reply and to which I have
never been able to find the answer.

When she spoke to me, I tried my best to reply but words failed,
because I am unused to being asked such questions, because my
head was full of the sad and angry man who attacked the statue,

the person who once loved me, the pictures I love and fear most in this gallery, and all the ghosts who have come today. I could not speak because I was already off duty, because I am unused to speaking, because I am a Warder at the Gallery of National Art.

JENNY GREENTEETH

♦ ♠ ♥ ♣

WERE YOU TO look at a map of the northeastern shore of Europe, and then look north from that shore, you might—if your eyes were strong enough—see a speck of green in the blue. And were you to find this speck, you would be forgiven for thinking it but a blemish, a drop of ink spilt by a former owner of the map, or a small mistake on the part of the cartographer or printer. But were you to look again, more carefully this time, you would see neither misprint nor stain, but an island.

A careless mapmaker may have ignored this island completely, believing such a tiny speck would not be missed by anyone, but exist it does—on a reputable map, at least, a dark green pinpoint amid the pale blue. And were you to take a boat there, over the cold, flat sea, it would no longer be a mere mark on paper, but would take body, become sheer physical heft, and seem vast: rock, grass, and soil extending as far as your eye could see before again becoming one with water, sky, and wind.

Of those few who lived on that island, some considered themselves Swedes, others Finns, others German, and some Pomeranian. Were they to argue, which they rarely did, they would have agreed that they were Baltic folk, more of the water than the land, knowing the sea connected rather than divided them from the countries that circled. Their island was so small, no nation would have risked much to claim it, and so its grass had been left to grow, its tides to rise and fall, its inhabitants to inhabit, and its rocks to slowly become sand, then slip back into the sea, as shall we all.

This is what Paul would have said were anyone to ask him, though few did, because the island people were taciturn, and Paul's opportunities for conversation were limited because he lived alone and took his boat out for much of each day. He set out early and returned late to sell his catch or work on the never-ending maintenance of the boat and his house, making sure each was caulked, stable, and watertight. The sea was rising, he was convinced, or the land was sinking; it mattered little either way, and he would tell anyone this as he sold them sprat or flounder or plaice, or helped them, in turn, to tar a roof or keel, or ferry something from one end of the island to the other. Once this island had been part of the land, he'd say, but the sea had won, and they would listen to him, and nod, and say nothing, because everyone knew Paul was kind but strange, the only child of a German couple who'd moved here during the boom, then both died, one after the other, just as soon as the boy was able to take care of himself. Paul never thought of returning; for him, there was no *return*—he had grown up here, and this flat island was his home, and here he would stay, he told the postmaster, or Samuel with the cows, or the other boatmen, and they would listen and nod and scarcely believe him, for even though they all acknowledged that Paul knew the island like no one else, and the sea around it, and was a good man, he was not from here, and he was not nor ever would be really, truly one of them.

They had come during the boom, his parents, some thirty or forty years back, no one remembered exactly when, and time slipped by so strangely on the island that counting years seemed a pointless occupation. A German poet had visited and written a poem about the almost-sunset of midsummer, the strange light and the sound of gulls, and the island had become briefly famous, though it was said the poet had been haughty, and was more known for a ribald limerick he'd also written while visiting about how a woman from the island would never marry because she smelled of fish, but it hadn't mattered, it had been enough, the tourists had begun to arrive, shiploads of them at the peak of the boom, mostly green-looking from the journey, no matter how calm the sea, and they were loaded onto a cart, covered in blankets and furs, the richer ones, then taken into the town, which had begun to grow in the deepwater cove on the more shel-tered western coast. Post began to arrive regularly on an official yellow-and-blue-painted boat, a postmaster was installed, post-cards were sold. A widow let out her superfluous rooms, and soon the Widow's House became known as the island's only hotel, even after the widow herself died. Its dining room grew famous for its stockfish broth. A ferry company opened a weekly route in the summer, twice-monthly during the winter. There had been talk of a Kurhaus, and some Germans had come, and made plans, and dug foundations, and even constructed part of the first floor, but no more. It was said that a war had got in the way, or something, but no one on the island knew much of it. Little touched them, apart from the wind.

Some days, when the weather would not let him take his boat out, Paul made anxious circuits of the coast on foot, looking for an inlet where the water was calmer or a higher point from where he would have vantage to see farther into the sky, and spot a distant break in the clouds, which predicted later calm. He often passed the quarter-built spa hotel, its never-used iron balustrade rusting in the salty wind. They had chosen the wrong location, he told people: Even though it was convenient for the harbour, this eastern coast was too exposed, its long shores of pebble and sand mere proxy for water and wind. Better to have chosen the other side of the island, gnarled and rocky, one of the low cliffs where the land had reared up out of the water as if a dog snarling at the waves, and tamed and becalmed it.

At the southern tip, thick grass grew as far as the sea itself, the fields becoming the sea, reaching back for the mainland to which they had once been joined. Cows wandered the shore, some belonging to Samuel, others to anyone who would milk them. The opposite point was a flinty arrowhead pointing due north, a long outcrop where a man could stand and watch the sky turn green.

All this, supposed Paul aloud, to himself if no one else were around, was what attracted the artists who had continued to come in their dribs and drabs even when the boom had died away, all this earth, water, air, light. Sometimes he'd watch them, setting up easels on the shore and finding themselves surprised by a sudden tide and having to up sticks and run before the water took them, or sitting under a tree with a large sketchbook perched on their knees, some with oils, some watercolours, others nothing but charcoal. He always wanted to see what they were doing, so he asked politely. Some would bat him away, but others were happy to share, so he'd look at their poorly rendered seas and watery skies, the endless pictures of the long barns and low houses that seemed to fascinate them so. They came in clumps, little groups that sometimes stuck together and other times dispersed. They usually stayed in one of the houses they painted, a house that became known as the Colony. They never stayed long, though. A month, two, three at the most. Paul had asked one, once, if she were planning to stay, and the woman said no, because even though the days here in the middle of the summer seemed to last as long as the summer itself, the light was too particular, too strange, and the water, she said, well, the water would freeze your bones, no matter what the season. It was true, Paul agreed, though he knew that these were precisely two of the reasons why he so wished to stay here.

They asked him, sometimes, to carry their things for them, their easels and canvases and oversized sketchbooks and boxes of pencils and paints, their bags and blankets and baskets of sandwiches and bottles of wine. Tracks across the island were few, and on a calm summer day, it was far easier to load everything into Paul's boat and ferry them from one spot to another. Usually Paul would do this for a group of them, and then take the painters, too, and sometimes their companions as well, should they wish to come, even a dog, perhaps, the load of them making a merry crew, but once it happened that a single man asked him for help.

Ellis, he said when Paul asked his name, and Paul said that was a strange name, and the man said, yes, it was a strange name. I was named for my mother, he said, it was her surname, and they gave it to me. She was English, so I suppose I'm part English, too, and perhaps that's why I talk strange. Paul soon discovered that the man didn't talk much at all, strange or not, though he found himself immediately at comfort with the man's silence as they loaded a bag and an easel onto the boat and pushed off into the water. Ellis seemed to know where he was going even though he said he'd never visited the island before. He stood at the prow, pointing directions and asking questions about the land. Always the land, never the sea. They eventually moored at a point toward the north of the island, not at the famous spit that Paul had assumed Ellis had wanted but a bland point farther in, where nothing but low fields rolled away as far as the western coast. No barns, no houses, no cows, even.

When Ellis set up his canvas, Paul was surprised by the fact that he had his back to the sea. He wanted to tell Ellis that he was facing the wrong way, that he should turn around, that all the artists painted the shore, and the sea, and the clouds over the sea, not empty fields. He offered to take him a little farther up, where a cluster of fishing huts and smokehouses huddled in the lee of the last rock before the island ended, a good spot that not many had painted before, said Paul, but no, Ellis wanted none of that, stood where he was, looked inland, and began his day's work.

When Paul returned that evening, Ellis didn't seem to have done much. The canvas was largely empty, a few streaks of green, and yellow, and blue, and greenish-yellow, and greenish-blue only, traversing the white space. Paul assumed Ellis was having trouble, though the painter seemed content with his work as they wrapped it carefully, then loaded it back onto the boat and headed south again.

"Are you at the Colony?" asked Paul.

"The where?" replied Ellis.

"The Colony. Where all the artists stay."

"I haven't heard of that, no."

Ellis seemed disinclined to talk further, and they passed the rest of the journey in silence, until they reached the spot where Paul had picked him up that morning. Paul jumped into the shallows and dragged the boat ashore, then helped Ellis carry his bags to his lodgings, and he did the same thing the next day, and the one after that, and the one after that. Each afternoon, Paul would arrive and look at what Ellis had done, and he saw little. The canvases seemed almost empty to him, bare save for a few swashes of colour. The artist always stood with his back to the sea, looking inward across the featureless ground.

"What do you think?" asked Ellis on the third day.

"I'm not sure," said Paul.

"Look carefully," said Ellis. "If you look carefully, you should be able to see the sea beyond." So Paul looked carefully, and he saw.

That evening as they were returning, Ellis told Paul he had only paid for three days' lodgings and needed somewhere to stay.

Paul had inherited the house from his parents, a long flat building with a high sloped roof that stood on the firmer, drier edge of a marsh and had a brook winding around it. It had been a barn, he told Ellis (though in truth he wasn't sure), adapted by one of the people who came over with the boom, or possibly a farmhouse whose owner had moved back to the mainland after finding the conditions too difficult out here. Paul had tarred the roof, time and again, and replaced the window frames when they began to let in too much wind, but had done little else, and over the next few years Ellis did much more, fixing the pump, the tiled floor, a warped door frame. Ellis was better that way, better with his hands, more practical, dextrous. Paul was a sailor, after all, a man who knew about water and wind; Ellis was a craftsman, a knower of the tangible, the solidity of stone and wood.

Ellis found bits of work to earn money, his skills useful on an island where most things apart from rain and wind were in short supply. He became known, liked, a quiet man, reliable. Sometimes he would crate up one or more of his pictures, and take them to the postmaster, and have them sent back to the mainland, where, Paul assumed, they would be sold or displayed in galleries, but he never really knew because Ellis talked little of it. "Once the work is done I have little further interest in it," was all he'd ever say. He painted a picture of the brook and told Paul he'd done it because he was fascinated by the way you could never tell which way it was flowing. He didn't send that one away, but hung it on the wall next to the window that looked out onto the brook the painting depicted. It was the only one of his pictures they kept.

They spent days together, silence never falling as they found the island filled with noises, birdcalls, grass in wind, rocks skittering over themselves, the sea. They spent days apart, Ellis on the land, Paul on the sea.

"The sea's like time," said Paul, because now he had someone to listen to him. "Time's not a river, a river will tell you little, but if you listen to the sea, and observe it, really, really carefully, you'll find all the currents and eddies and tides, some hardly visible. There are endless depths, piled on one another. There are creatures, I've read, who live so deep in the sea no man has ever seen them."

"It's so cold," said Ellis, "the water here. The land has warmth in it, it holds time. When you learn to read it, it's like a book."

"It can preserve things forever, this cold water," said Peter. "You could live forever, as long as you didn't mind being dead."

One thing only disturbed them. One day, Ellis, at home alone, searching for a box, or paper, or something, he couldn't remember what, or later even why he'd been looking, chanced on a pile of notebooks.

"I didn't know you wrote," he told Paul on his return.

"You didn't think I could?"

"No," replied Ellis, "not that. I didn't mean that."

"Did you read them?" asked Paul.

"No," said Ellis. "I didn't," and he hadn't.

In winter, storm was a constant. Weather kept a dark grip on the island, loosening its hold for a few days here and there, turning bright and glacial before black wind and ice returned. In midsummer, however, storm was a freak that could come from nowhere, and although people were prepared, each time was new.

Wrecks were rare, but not unknown. Most shores were soft here, and low, and there was no spectacular breaking, but more often a running aground, ships left beleed, tilted, or upended, unable to move for days, weeks sometimes, until tides and currents and winds had changed. Storm could bring a ship ashore, or take it away again.

One evening, midsummer, around the time of the notebooks, the air was bright but stifling, and a sulphurous dimness settled toward midnight. Paul had seen such nights before, waiting until the worst had passed before taking his own boat out to help, should it be necessary, and called on Ellis to look out with him. Instead of the moment when darkness almost fell, when day and night each lost focus, tonight it was the line between sky and sea that became indistinguishable. The air flashed cold and bitter. Ellis looked aghast at the waves, which seemed of a curious substance, like jellyfish washing up on the shore. A crowd formed around them, lanterns swinging. Paul helped the other boatmen lash down tarpaulins. Some thought they could see a ship, dashed between the waves, vying with the indistinct horizon. Others said there was nothing there, that it was but a trick played by the lightning, or the waves themselves turning on one another. Those still sleeping were woken by a new, swiftly approaching roar, amazed their sea could sing now in this voice. A pillar of salt foam whirled sky high, then fell back into the sea. Then the air flashed again and, as if obeying its signal, the voice died away. The waves calmed. The small crowd assured each other the night was safe again, wished each other good sleep, and dispersed.

The next morning was clear, though the air was still suffused with salt and ozone, as if scrubbed, and Paul went out early to check on his boat, hoping for little damage and a good catch. Storms brought fish. It was the lightning, Paul claimed, which drew them to the surface.

Later, if asked, which for a while he frequently was, Paul wouldn't really remember if Jenny had been lying on the shore, or standing there as if waiting for him, or merely sitting on the upturned boats. The latter seemed most likely, and thus became the story he told.

A woman, his own age, perhaps a little older, perhaps a little younger, was sitting on his upturned boat. She was cold, so very cold, and pale, and had a small cut on her forehead that had stopped bleeding because it was so cold. Paul would then add the detail of kelp or bladderwrack being tangled in her sodden coat or hair, but soon he wouldn't be able to remember if that were true or not.

Paul led her up to the house, where Ellis waited at the doorway.

"Hello," she said to Ellis in English, as if she knew him already, and he welcomed her in, and brewed tea, and found her a dry, warm blanket, one which he had hung next to the fire as if he'd been waiting for her, and Jenny had arrived, and it is here that this story might begin.

C. D. ROSE

She had hair that changed colour with the light: sometimes it was that of sand, sometimes that of rock. Her eyes flashed green into blue into grey—the sea, obviously. She had bits of several languages, German, French, Swedish, but not much of any at first until she grew into remembering, or learning, more. No one knew if she'd come from the ship that night or not, or even if there'd been a ship. She remembered nothing other than arriving on the shore that morning.

The cut above her eye soon healed, and she soon grew warm. It was the middle of summer, after all. They found her a bed, and she stayed.

She said her name was Jenny but nothing more. Paul called her Pirate Jenny because she had arrived in a boat and stolen his heart. Ellis called her Jenny Greenteeth because he remembered a story his mother had told him about a woman who lived in the water.

Jenny told them she had been born in Sweden, or Germany, or Russia, and had lived in France, and Holland, and Denmark, that she had been a governess to two naughty children in Belgium, a lady's maid in England, and an artist's model in Vienna, and Ellis and Paul listened and did not believe her, but it mattered little. Her tales were the stuff of fiction and, like the best stories, illuminated their lives in ways they hadn't imagined.

The temperature rose when she arrived, the coolness of the summer evenings dispelled in favour of a slow warmth that stayed in the house like a cat. Light softened at the edges, finding new corners to brighten. When winter arrived, such light lengthened the days, and the warmth turned the darkness into a thick blanket. When spring came around, Jenny went out more, and returned bearing bunches of bright blue flax, coarse yellow dandelions, towering lupins, or buttery cow-wheat, and once, a lush purple marsh orchid.

In the town, some noted how kind Paul was, taking in orphans and waifs like he did. Others thought he had opened a hotel, or a boardinghouse, while others speculated on which man was the woman's lover, and some said it was both of them, because they were all foreign, and one was an artist. Some said no good would come of a woman from the sea, but both Ellis and Paul knew her no creature; she was too human. While Paul cooked and Ellis cleaned, Jenny threw her coat on the floor and her scarf on the stove, dropped shoes in the fireplace, trampled mud and dirt into the kitchen, left teacups on the floor and strands of her hair in the sink. Paul washed plates, and Jenny broke them. Ellis swabbed the floor, and Jenny left footprints on it.

Jenny remembered nothing but the names of flowers, and music. Although she had spoken little at first, Paul and Ellis quickly grew used to her constantly tapping out rhythms on tabletops, or moving her feet in time to some unheard melody, or singing snatches of songs that themselves sounded rescued from the deeps. Jenny, Paul wrote and Ellis thought, aspired to the condition of music.

One fragment repeated itself, a few notes of an air, each time in a different key, sometimes slowly, others more quickly, sometimes repeating, other times fading into nothing after a few bars. One night toward midsummer, a year after she had arrived, when the light had a spectral edge and even the sea seemed to be sleeping, the pieces came together as Jenny sat on the doorstep looking out across the island and began to sing. The song had no words, or none that either Ellis or Paul recognised, and none she would later be able to recall, but a melody that seemed snatched from the wind, as old as the rocks, as deep as the sea and as fragile as the petals of the flowers she gathered.

"It's called 'The Blind Accordionist,'" she said, though she did not know why, or where the song had come from, or where she had ever heard it, or who had ever sung or played it to her.

Were anyone to see one, two, or the three of them in the town or crossing a field or walking the shore, they would notice how Paul was now less talkative but Ellis more so, and while Jenny was strange, certainly, who wasn't who had landed on these shores? She had found land, people said, and would stay there, anchored.

Years passed. Years. None of them could remember how many; none of them kept tally. It was like the small river that ran around their house—no one could tell if it flowed to the left, or the right. The sea lay in either direction, after all. The three of them were a piece of music, a trio moving slowly in and out of time, so slowly no mortal ear could perceive the music, only someone able to listen for centuries.

Were you to peer in at their window of a night, you would see them, Ellis fixing a loose tile or warped floorboard, Paul writing, Jenny being music, and you would think of happiness, but were you to look again, more carefully, perhaps, you would see things that these people themselves did not know, like blemishes on a map that turned out to be real places, like water creeping in under a house, like the salt that slowly eroded everything here, like the tiny signs Paul could see of approaching storm, or the gradation of light and colour only Ellis knew.

Of Jenny, we knew nothing. She told us nothing. She told so little to anyone else in this story, and men, so often, have such little understanding of women. *Man to the hills, woman to the shore*, they'd say, but Jenny was clearly of neither, or both. Yet we should not think her without agency. Jenny had a soul, and a big one, though we shall not know it, perhaps, until later, or not at all.

Paul and Ellis believed Jenny had brought a truce between sea and sky and land. Since she had arrived, they noted, there had been no more storms, not even in winter, nothing more than a few spats between the elements.

And then, one day, she told them she was leaving.

They were sitting around the table finishing a dinner of herring and potatoes, of which Jenny had not taken a bite.

"The wind here has blown through the very flesh and bones of me," she told them. "My heart and spirit have been dried and salted. I cannot be the oil for your lives. What am I to do here? To end up stinking of fish?"

A mailboat carrying a group of German tourists was to leave for the mainland the next morning. Jenny packed a bag and left.

The next night, surely enough, a storm howled. The tide rose so high Paul scooped fish from the back step. Ellis lay in bed and didn't paint or fix anything. The two men didn't speak to one another. Of the boat that had left for the mainland, there was no news.

When the storm eventually lulled, Paul was not convinced: he knew that sulphurous dimness, the strange vibration of air that belied the clear sky. Again toward midnight, a huge bank of cloud rolled in like a vengeful locomotive, its thunder that of iron striking iron. The very sky seemed to crack open, revealing a dazzling white light beyond. The sea rose, and sang bitterly.

Men swathed in oilcloth and carrying lanterns came to the house.

"There's a ship," they shouted to Paul. "It's grounded at the spit. We'll need help."

"I can't take the boat, not tonight."

"Then leave it," they told him. "And bring Ellis. We need hands."

But Paul had his boots on already, and knew Ellis wanted nothing of the water, and knew too that they hadn't spoken for a day. He grabbed his sea coat and headed out with the men following the shore path to the north, and he didn't call Ellis, and he didn't look back.

When they arrived, the sky had retreated into a sullen bruise of clouds, tinged yellow and orange with swells of anger. Early dawn, this time of year.

"There it is," they shouted, the light from their stilled lamps now useless against the breaking morning. The rocky promontory was covered in splinters, matchsticks, firewood. It was hard to believe they had once formed a boat, though a chunk of hull remained. Paul recognised the blue and yellow paint on its clinkered beams. He moved closer. Three figures curled into its shelter, pale as fish skins, all drowned.

Paul collapsed onto a sodden mailsack. The others came to cover the faces of the dead.

"The Germans?" asked one.

"I think so," said another.

"Not Jenny?" asked Paul, and they shook their heads, and Paul breathed. They scoured the rocks and found two more bodies skeltered amid the debris. They picked them up, and stinking green water vomited from them. Neither was Jenny.

"The lifeboat?"

"No trace."

"It must have left before they wrecked."

"Hope?"

No one answered. The men relit their lamps and placed them on the rocks, as they had no candles to leave.

Back in the town, the men poured brandy into one another until they could feign a semblance of life. It took another day before Paul was ready to return home. He set foot out of the post office where they had retired, and there, on the threshold, as if waiting for him, stood Jenny.

Later, when he had drunk more brandy, and he had touched her face, and found her not to be a ghost, and realised that he, too, had not died, she told him.

"I couldn't leave," she said. "I was ready for the boat, but I couldn't. I didn't know what to do. I thought I was trapped, but then saw I wasn't. I stayed at the Widow's House. I was going to come back, I was, I promise. I'll always come back. This water has seeped into me. This wind has shaped and sculpted me. This place has become me. And you, too. How could I be without you and Ellis?"

It was a quiet calm morning, finally, clear skies and the buzz of ozone and the scour of salt. Bright blue and yellow flowers lifted their heads again. The island sang. It would be a good morning for fish, Paul told her as they walked back home.

Jenny sang, too, more loudly than the land itself, but Paul told her not to, as that would convince Ellis he was haunted, so they laughed instead and shouted his name as they approached.

Ellis didn't come to the door to see what the noise was. They went to the bedroom, but the bed was empty. He'll have gone out painting, they told each other, a day like this. So they went to look for him, by the shore, looking inland, but he wasn't there, and he wasn't in the field either, and they walked farther, but he wasn't there, or there, or there.

They went back to the town, because—obviously—Ellis would have gone there to find Paul, because Ellis would have worried. They would find him, surely, sitting in the post office, or eating soup at the Widow's House.

When they got to the quay, they saw Paul's boat moored there. Paul felt a cold shadow cross his path. The boat shouldn't be here, at the quay. It was out of place. Paul hadn't noticed it missing from its usual mooring, what with the chaos of the night, and didn't understand why it was here now. His boat was empty.

One of the other men had towed it back in, to this side of the island, empty.

"It must have been the storm," he said. "The storm must have dragged it out," he said, full knowing his boat was always tethered so firmly the strongest of winds couldn't take it. "The storm," he said. "It must have been the storm." But it hadn't been the storm, and he knew it hadn't.

"Ellis," they told him. "Last night. After you'd gone. Ellis took it out. He wanted to find you. He went after you. We found it drifting, this morning, after you'd left."

Ellis had taken the boat, Paul's boat, Ellis who never went to sea, the night Paul had chosen the land because he knew the water was treacherous.

"Hope?" he asked, and no one replied.

And here we could talk of the passing of time, but time did not pass for them. Time folded into itself. Paul told himself the story over and over and over again, to get its details right, to think of the forks and turns of it, to think of how it could be told differently and reach a different ending, then rued the treachery of the story itself, which always came to the same conclusion, no matter how many possibilities it offered. Jenny stopped singing. Paul and Jenny did not even notice each other grow older, only slower, perhaps, a grey hair or wrinkle appearing, but this seemed nothing more than a cloud passing, or driftwood washing up on the shore. They thought of the years, *years*, they had passed together, and they were nothing more than minutes, all that memory compressed into a few moments of sensation that had impressed themselves onto their minds like the burn of lightning. The immensity of their experience did not escape them; a sense of scale did. This story is nothing but a tiny speck on a vast map, a mere blemish in the eye of the creator.

Little changed on the island. Life happened. They heard of wars, of countries being formed, then no longer existing. Maps were redrawn. They heard of the spread of railways, the invention of the telegraph. A French photographer came and took pictures of the town and its inhabitants, but not of Paul or Jenny. Bigger ships began to arrive, taking advantage of the deep, cold water. The tide came in and went out; the wind blew; the grass grew, and the cows ate it. Paul and Jenny lived alone for the next forty years. Bushes grew from the eaves of the house, buckets placed to catch the drips from the leaking roof rusted, the whole place slouched, making its own unspoken accommodation with the wind. Some days they passed together, others apart. Jenny still gathered flowers, and sometimes, when she believed herself alone, sang, the wind her only harmony, her songs without metre or time, and any melody as slow as the land. Paul's boat let in water, and his beard grew. He continued to fish or to carry when he could.

At this point, there should have been a third storm, but there wasn't, although Paul would later remember the sulphurous light, the green ray. It was one of the new ships, the big ones Paul had seen in the offing or up close, looming over the small port. Too big to sink, they'd said, so big you wouldn't even know you were on a ship, with huge nets that could rake the depths. It had docked with a strange cargo: tangled amid the silvery thrash and heave of its trawl, a young man, drowned, quite dead. At first they'd thought him one of the crew, gone overboard, a terrible accident, such things happen, but once laid on a slab, they saw he wasn't, and word went around, and they called on Paul and Jenny.

And there he was, as pale and beautiful as the last dawn they'd seen him: Ellis, still dressed in the only coat he had, as if sleeping.

"He must be cold, he must be so cold," said Paul when he saw him, and pulled a blanket over his face.

When they laid Ellis's body in the shifting ground, Paul wore his Sunday best, and Jenny sang a song no one recognised but everyone felt they knew.

I heard this story from my father, but I never believed it, and now he is dead, too.

SOSIA AND THE CAPTAIN

———— ♦ ♠ ♥ ♣ ————

"COINCIDENCE IS INDEED a strange thing," said the lawyer, in the dining room of a hotel in a town that, in all honesty, had seen better days, following up a tale told by someone I've now quite forgotten, about another chance encounter or unexpected recognition. "I once heard this story about a young woman, somewhere in France, I believe," he continued, being a man who liked the sound of his own voice but who was nevertheless interesting, "who'd discovered her husband was having an affair, and decided in her grief and distraction to throw herself off the top of a parapet. She did so, and on landing hit the errant husband on his way back into their house, killing him stone dead. She survived, I believe, though I have no idea what then became of her."

"A fine tale indeed, but it surely never happened," replied one of his fellow diners. "Some piece of gossip or tittle-tattle, something fashioned for the mere sake of a barroom anecdote."

"It surely did, Sir," replied the lawyer, who was my brother. "I read of it in a newspaper and have kept the illustration." He had, it is true. He kept a large collection of cuttings of such unlikely tales, and their gruesome illustrations, in several languages.

"An illustration?" retorted the sceptic. "The handiwork of an overheated, underpaid mind, I shouldn't wonder. Now, if there were a *photograph* . . ."

The conversation turned to the various merits of the art of photography (and, indeed, if it were even worthy of being called an "art") and its pretensions (or otherwise) to truth (and, therefore, beauty) before turning back in on itself (as conversations involving my brother the lawyer were wont to do) to consider the nature of coincidence once again, and its role in photography, photography being the very "coincidence of time, place, and light," as one gentleman (myself) suggested.

"But this is not a story about coincidence," interrupted a voice from the back of the room, the voice of someone who, up until now, had been quietly seated alone, taking little apparent notice of us gabbling topers. Though the voice was deep, its lilt suggested something other to us, and as we turned to look, we noted that what we had, from the corner of our eyes, taken to be merely yet another solitary gent was in fact a woman—a rather mannishly dressed one, perhaps, but notably handsome—in her later middle years. "Not coincidence, no, nor irony, nor tragedy. It's a story about love."

"Love?" asked the lawyer.

The woman nodded.

"And what form of love would that be?"

"Love takes many forms," she said, "but there is only one way to speak of it."

The lady was invited to join us, but declined and continued her speech from where she sat. Despite having remained near invisible for most of the evening, the woman was, it seemed, rather used to being able to command attention when necessary, as we all found ourselves turning toward her as if we were heliotropic plants.

"Your story is most interesting," she continued, scarcely moving her glass of brandy or raising her voice, "and though I cannot vouch for its authenticity, the truth is that such things happen more often than we may care to admit."

"It sounds very much like you have your own story to tell," said someone (possibly myself).

"The story is, I own, in its way, rather similar to a story in which I once found myself a participant."

"And what story would that be?"

She paused, and took another sip of the brandy. "It's all so long ago now," she said. "I'm not quite sure I can remember it all." But we were primed and implored her to continue, and she did.

"I was in Paris," she began, and we settled, and we listened. "I travelled widely in those days, unlike now, when I am so much more limited. I was passing one of those riverbank *bouquinistes* when my eye happened to be caught by a particular photograph on sale. Upon closer inspection it turned out it was not exactly a photograph but a very carefully pencilled drawing. I had a professional interest, you see. Back then, I was a practising photographer. An unusual profession for a woman, certainly, if it was indeed a 'profession' at all—needless to say, I made a scant living from it—but an unusual profession for anyone in those days, though it was already burgeoning, even back then.

"The picture that had piqued my curiosity was that of what appeared to be an opera singer, a slender yet full-throated woman in an extravagant gown and clutching an even more extravagant bouquet in the act of taking a bow, having triumphantly acquitted her role as Violetta, or Marguerite, or Eurydice, perhaps.

"I asked the vendor who the drawing depicted and was greeted with some surprise. *Why,* said the little man in a tone of astonishment, *it is Frieda Capgras!* I had never heard of the woman, and told him so, only to be informed that she was currently the *étoile* of the entire city, making me feel somewhat the ignorant foreigner. I immediately purchased the print and asked him if he had any other images of the woman, but he told me they were selling so quickly it was impossible to get hold of more. Before he could say anything else, I slipped the picture into my bag and made off, having already resolved to find this woman as soon as was humanly possible.

"You are wondering, of course, what had intrigued me so about this picture, and what had made me take such a course of action. The reason is a strange one, and I scarce believe it myself, even now. When I saw that picture that day, I was amazed, because *I was looking at myself.* Famous opera singer Frieda Capgras was *the exact image of me*, identical, indistinguishable. Two drops of water could not have been more similar. Despite her flamboyant attire, her features spoke—the line of the jawbone, the arch of the brow, the prominence of the nose, and the lips set like a stormy horizon . . . This was *my* face, my physiognomy, my *self*. The effect was astonishing, to the extent that I found myself briefly wondering if I had ever sung in an opera and been feted for my performance, despite full well knowing that no such thing had ever occurred.

"I made enquiries and found that she was due to sing again in a week's time, at the Palais Garnier, no less, but not a single ticket was available and no amount of money or influence would be enough to procure one. I tried to find out where she was staying, if she were resident in Paris or, like myself, a visitor to the city, but was told that her whereabouts were a closely kept secret, and that she guarded her privacy fiercely. Many admirers had pursued her, all in vain—not because they had been rebuffed, merely because they had failed to find her.

"In the meantime, as sometimes happens when one chances across a hitherto unknown word or phrase or idea and begins to see it everywhere, I found I could not escape from La Capgras. Her image stared at me from bills pasted to walls, from the covers of the *Petit* or the *Siècle* or other collections of *faits divers* that populated the newsstands, or from postcards that I bought whenever I saw them. And whether painted or drawn or gravured, and whether in the role of farmgirl, princess, or ancient divinity, no matter how her hair had been arranged or what outlandish makeup she wore, she was always, always identical to me.

"The week passed, and I decided to go to the theatre anyway, and to loiter by the artists' entrance. Although the street was murky, a significant crowd had already gathered. No one saw anyone entering or leaving, and yet, from inside, word emerged that Capgras had taken the stage. The same eerie thing happened at the end of the performance—even from outside, we could hear the thunder of applause, the cries, the cheers, the whistles, and we waited, for hours, it seemed, for even a single figure to emerge, until all the lights of the house had gone dark, but none came. It was only when the crowd of well-wishers had begun to disperse, disconsolate, that I noticed a small, shambling figure wearing the ill-fitting uniform of a concierge seem to lock the door of a storage cellar and merge into the night. The figure walked with exactly the same gait as mine.

"Capgras had no further engagements in the capital, though the papers announced a tour with appearances in Biarritz, Nice, Lausanne, Baden-Baden, and Karlovy Vary. I eventually tracked her down in Milan, a bleak place at its best, though the fog there is rather special.

"Though of the gentler sex, I am not without my wiles, so forewent the opportunity to see her sing and instead gave a small favour to a friendly *maschera* who in turn handed me the key to La Capgras's dressing room. Yes—when one is truly determined, almost anything can be achieved. I sat and waited, listening to her—finally!—as her voice trailed through the winding backstage corridors, as enchanting as night, at once aethereal and corporeal. Such a sound I had never heard before, and, to be frank, never have since.

"When eventually the applause and calls for yet another encore died away, the door burst open and she entered alone, a cloud of perfume and silk, the odour of her perspiration and heavy stage makeup distinct beneath it. She seemed unsurprised to find me waiting, as if dressing room intruders were a commonplace—which, perhaps, they were—or, knowing what I would come to know later, as if she had been waiting for me all along.

"I myself, on the other hand, was astonished. I could almost have been looking in a mirror. Although I had seen her likeness, pictures are often heavily tinted or pencilled, and I wasn't prepared for her actual appearance. The possibility of twinship, that La Capgras and I had somehow been separated at birth, had, of course, occurred to me as soon as I first saw her picture, though my family circumstances being what they were—another story, one which we do not have time for now—I knew this an impossibility. And now that I saw, I could see that we were not *quite* identical: She was younger than me. Only by a few months—a year, perhaps, no more—but she definitely retained a flush of juvenescence that I, alas, had lost.

"She sat at her dressing table and hurriedly began to remove her makeup while almost casually asking who I was. I began to tell her my name but immediately found myself struck by a kind of stammer, which has from time to time afflicted me since my early youth. To explain: My given name is Cecilia, but as a child—due to this impediment, or perhaps mere childish verbal stumbling—I found the name, my own name, difficult to pronounce, and instead came out with an approximative *Sosia*. The name has stuck to me ever since.

"'Sosia,' she said, flatly, without surprise, as though trying the word out in her mouth. It seemed to please her. 'Welcome! My name, as you must know, is Frieda Capgras, but also Letizia

Shartz-Metterklume, and sometimes Mathilde Schwob, though I have also been called Jane Shore, Jára Cimrman, Pierre André-zel, and—once—Elsa Plötz.' As she listed her names, she hastily undid her gown and began rummaging in a voluminous canvas travelling bag from which she whisked a military uniform, its nation and rank unfamiliar to me, then slipped it on as easily as a shift. 'But you, Sosia my dear,' she continued, 'may call me—the Captain!' She saluted, and I saluted back, having no other idea of what to do. 'When in trouble,' she proclaimed, 'or when in doubt, or when in time of difficulty—pretend to be someone else!' We stole out of the back of the theatre and I, of course, was immediately enamoured.

"It was a ruse, she claimed, as we hurried through fog-lined streets, to avoid the mass of her adoring fans, many of whom could be positively tedious, if not worse. We soon found ourselves in a cab, and then, not long after, in a shabby hotel somewhere on the road to Lodi. It was the kind of place I would become familiar with over the next few months, as we made our way through the flat hinterlands of northeastern Italy, subsisting on dishes of sloppy rice and boiled chicory served up in railway station cafés and roadside *osterie*. I had never, I thought, been so happy in my life. I had always wanted a life of adventure, and now one was being handed to me.

"In Treviso, we posed as twin sisters from an aristocratic family, inventing our own private language for the whole evening to conceal our origins from a generous admirer. In Rovigo, we had to spend the night under a hedge after the Captain believed she had been spotted. In Bassano del Grappa, we had to escape in a hurry when the aforementioned generous admirer's pocketbook was discovered in one of the Captain's many travelling bags by an overcurious laundrymaid. Despite her fame, the Captain had much to conceal, it seemed.

"It was only when we reached Venice that she seemed to achieve some form of tranquillity. She was due to sing again, and this always gave her peace. Only when performing, perhaps, could she be her true self—though what that true self might have been, I was never quite sure. It was during our stay in La Serenissima that she finally began to tell me something of herself. She *was* a singer, of course, a divine one, but that, she told me, was not her real vocation, merely a mask to cover her true profession: the Captain was a spy.

"I wasn't taken aback by her revelation. Things began to make sense. Not only her capacity for disguise and the rapidity with which she accomplished it, nor her constant worry about being found out, but mostly—I own—the mystery about the contents of her travelling bags. We had, after all, managed to adventure all this way in near-constant possession of her numerous valises, suitcases, Gladstones, satchels, clutches, and carpetbags. Apart from the few occasions when she had trusted someone enough to take them on for us, she had never let her collection leave her sight. It was only in Venice that I was allowed to explore the riot of costumery and millinery they contained: stage costumes fashioned from peacock feathers, sequins, and wonder; a quartermaster's store of military uniforms—dress *and* battle; one very large black overcoat that was big enough to house the both of us;

shoes ranging from the most delicate of ballet pumps to stout Oxfords to fiendishly high leather boots that would take an age to lace; two men's suits; bolero jackets of French satin and Florentine velvet; hooks and eyes; buttons, of pearl, of brass; masks.

"Given my profession, I of course wanted to photograph her, but this was forbidden. I only had to broach the idea of a portrait before it was immediately dismissed. 'I can never be photographed,' declaimed the Captain. 'Should they want to draw me, paint me, imagine me—well, I cannot stop them. But no one, no one ever, shall fix my image in light itself.' It was true: though I had by then seen many images of her, not one was a photograph, and though I tried to argue my case, my attempts were in vain. She was adamant that she must never, ever have her picture taken.

"On the evenings she was engaged, I was to drink chocolate in the small café opposite La Fenice, drawing the crowds away from her by attracting them to myself, only then to disappoint them when they realised I was a mere lookalike. At first, our plan didn't work—no one would believe *I* wasn't *she*, but when I hit upon the simple yet brutal idea of blacking out a front tooth with coloured sticking plaster, they rapidly came to their senses: my smile saw them run; La Capgras could have no imperfection. In the watery labyrinth of that city, all shimmer and shadow, it was easy to vanish, and we were able to spend many hours alone and undisturbed.

"We discovered that our similarities were not only physical. We had both been born into complex families—and what family isn't?

you may well ask, but ours, I believed, were more complex than most—and we had been moving ever since we were little. Neither of us had a native tongue; we were both born into many languages. Neither of us were ever at home, and we were both, perhaps, always fleeing from one. Neither of us had ever felt truly loved.

"'When I first saw you,' the Captain told me, 'I saw the double nature of the world, and how in the double, imagined aspects lie the pleasure and beauty of things. Everything is double. Everything has its companion.'

"One night, we were crossing some misty bridge or other when our story turned again: the Captain told me of another spy, a most subtle and dangerous one—the Blind Accordionist. Such was the sobriquet or alias or nickname of the said agent, and the Captain's mission was to track him down. It was only then I realised: the Captain was not fleeing, nor hiding—she was *chasing after!*

"And chase we did. A day later, her public obligations discharged, a message arrived at her poste restante, and we were moving again.

"In Prague, we posed as lady travellers and diarists to meet her contact, a man known as the Jackdaw who had a curious moustache and frequented the lowest taverns. In Vienna, we discovered the Jackdaw was not who he had pretended to be and narrowly escaped on a train to Budapest, which we abandoned at a lonely halt for a quick change and a jump back onto a train heading south. The journey was long, and with no apparent destination, and—as can happen on such occasions—it proved an occasion for the further exchange of tales, and secrets.

"The Captain's life, it turned out, was not double as much as triple, or quadruple, or perhaps even more. She wasn't in the pay of one master but was spying on behalf of several governments, agencies, and private individuals. Over time, she had double- and triple-crossed many of them, leaving her unsure as to exactly whom she was working for and, often, *why*. The only constant, it seemed, was her obsession with the Blind Accordionist. And when I asked who this person really was, she could say no more. I suspected that she didn't even know.

"It was when we arrived in Naples that things began to fall apart. The endless train had drawn its halt there, the end of the line. The Captain claimed she had friends at the San Carlo, so we made for the opera house immediately. When she sang, she claimed, she was invincible. When I sing, she said, my voice takes over, and I become the instrument. When I sing, the song sings me. I need to sing, she said.

"And she sang. How she sang! Nightingales fashioned from quicksilver would envy her, the dying swan fall silent in admiration. Time itself stopped when she sang.

"I have to say here that my own story was not, at that point, without its complications. I have said that I was a photographer—I still am—but this was a profession I only chanced upon later, after several previous attempts at a career. I began as a lady's maid, but soon progressed to being the governess for the lady's children after the previous incumbent ran away. I had to leave that position after I was falsely accused of the theft of a precious necklace—a necklace that, by the way, I had found to be most ugly—and then became an artist's model, and from that an artist myself, if we can consider photography an art—which, gentlemen, was where I came into your conversation to begin with. But I am digressing again, and it is growing late. I meant to say that I was, perhaps, not an easy person to love. My own history had been marked by disappearance, evasion, inconsistency—the very things that, as a photographer, I tried to battle. I am aware of the irony. Furthermore, the one person who I desired to photograph more than anything in the world denied me the very chance of doing so. I realise now how frustrated I must have been.

"I was saying that time stopped when the Captain sang—the problem being that when she stopped singing, time's flow ran ever harder. In Naples, time poured, a deluge. Her supposed 'friends' in the city had allowed her to sing only because, it turned out, her performance was to pay off a debt that the Captain had—according to them—accrued on her previous visit to the city, and despite the success of her performance, it seemed she no longer had the financial draw she had once had—too much time spying, not enough singing—and a substantial portion of the debt remained. She tried to pay off the balance by producing a diamond from her bags—I was astonished, had never seen it before—but it turned out that the diamond had been stolen—from the person to whom she was offering it.

"We were moving again, and this time quite definitely fleeing. The Captain maintained that if she were to find the Blind Accordionist, all our troubles would be solved—I imagined a handsome reward, perhaps, though she never mentioned such a thing. But the trail had gone cold. I no longer remember quite how long we journeyed, always running, now hares, no longer foxes. We travelled third class, or by mail coach. We were often mistaken for vagrants, and more than once narrowly avoided a workhouse. At some point, we found ourselves in a flyblown town where everyone seemed to be worried about a game of cards of which we could make neither head nor tail. The Captain claimed she had an engagement on a tiny island in the Baltic Sea, but when we got there, we found the opera house had never been built and spent a miserable week eating broth made from salted fish, and left reeking of it. She had another possible engagement in Lemberg, but we took the wrong train and ended up in a town neither of us knew. It was dark when we arrived, and both hotels claimed to be full, so we retired to a café that seemed to be named the 'Question Mark,' were it named anything at all—the only symbol on the sign hanging above the doorway being a *?* ' When we walked in, everyone there looked exactly like us.

"It was a strange evening. Everyone in the café, male or female, young or old, was our double, or triple, or quadruple. And yet, I remember feeling utterly unsurprised, as though it were the most normal thing in the world. I was not, I think now, entirely well. The constant travel, the anxiety of discovery, and the obsessive need for secrecy had claimed a heavy price on my health, and—in turn—on our friendship. After we had been ushered into a private dining room and eaten a dinner of pork sausage and sulphurous cabbage, the Captain turned to me and told me that it was time for us to separate. 'I no longer need a travelling companion,' she said. 'Indeed, you have become a hindrance to me. Everything has its companion, and everything has its opposite. There is no doubling that is not also a splitting. I can only find what I want if I am alone.' And with that, she got up, and vanished.

"I had wanted to make her love me by doing everything she wanted, and then I realised that what she had wanted was someone who did not love her.

"It would be many years before I saw her again. I had found myself back in Paris, having resumed my work as a photographer. I say 'found myself,' but I suppose I had made my way there, drawn by that memory of my first encounter with her. The work was lucrative enough, but life was far from indulgent. I had become a mask of myself. I kept my eyes carefully peeled whenever I passed a newspaper stand or kiosk but never saw anything of the Captain. Where she had gone, or who she even was now, I did not know. I took portraits for gentlemen, and sometimes my clients would say that I reminded them of someone, though they could never quite say who.

"One of my sitters asked me to come and take some pictures at a ball he and his friends were holding, a reserved affair in which everyone was to come in costume. The event was to take place in a large house in Saint-Cloud, on the outskirts of the city, and I—accompanied by my camera—was to be delivered by cab. I, too, was asked to wear a disguise, but I chose nothing more than the voluminous cape I wore when working and a pair of dark glasses I used to protect me from glare. I was asked to set up in a small anteroom equipped with adequate lighting from where I could observe the guests. They seemed to be wearing the entire contents of the Captain's travelling bags.

"I imagine you know where this story is going, don't you? You are not mistaken. A woman presented herself. She wore a mask of feathers and pearls, seemed a creature so exotic not even our most intrepid explorers had ever recorded her. And despite that, before I had even seen the buttons on her boots, I knew her immediately."

"And she too. I hadn't even had time to check the light gauge and set the focus before she spoke: 'It is you, isn't it? *You* are the Blind Accordionist!'

"I was not, though I wished I had been. To have been desired so.

"She looked at me proudly, challenging me to do my worst, the one thing she had always forbade of me.

"The moment of feeling passed more rapidly than the snap of the shutter. The light flashed, and with it, I gained clarity. Looking back, I see now that I had already long realised how wrong she had been: Things are not double, but multiple, endless. There were not two of us, there were millions of us. There may only be one form of love, but there are many ways to speak of it. I finally took her photograph, and in so doing, I fixed her, and I destroyed her.

"She left the room hurriedly, her mask having slipped.

"The story should end here, and I see you are tiring, gentlemen, but it is not so clear. Things rarely are. I have never seen her since, but that has not stopped my search. Having taken her picture once, I found I needed nothing more than to do it again. Only then, I think, will I be rid of her. Why, after all, do you think I am in this dreary place now? I am still looking for her."

With that, the woman who had called herself Sosia ended her story, and the room fell silent, even more silent than it had been. Summer was reaching its end, and light did not hold as it had before. We put out the candles and made our way, slowly, to bed.

DEAD JOHANN

— ♦ ♠ ♥ ♣ —

CROOKED GROUND, CROOKED water, crooked eye, crooked daughter. Plum tree, pear tree, name me, kiss me. Blind crow, button my boots; blind owl, count my teeth; blind man, sing my song. In the house there hides a room, in the room there stands a bed, in the bed there lies a man. One for salt, two for iron, three for blood, in the man there is no good.

There is salt. There is no water. There is blood, there are ashes, there are bones.

Speak of ghosts; they will come.

THE
VISITORS

◆ ♠ ♥ ♣

THEY CAME TOWARD the end of the summer, when the grass was parched and shadows stretched as far as the horizon. Autumn had stolen a march on the dog days; leaves as brittle as old tobacco crunched underfoot, and squirrels busied themselves burying fat acorns. The dirt track to the house was solid, and turning to dust. There was no sign of rain yet. The air itself was tired.

Some wanted to buy hats in town, others to take walks to the lake or woods, and a few contented themselves to stay in and drink the early pear brandy. They had come to help, but Elizabeth found their company stifling. She had quickly grown used to the house's stillness and emptiness but had not yet spent enough time alone listening to the creaks and sighs of the old wooden frame. She didn't know how many visitors there were; they never stayed in the same place for long enough for her to count, congregating in the drawing room or on the porch or even in the kitchen in twos, threes, fours, or larger groups, sometimes singly surprising her on the stair or in the scullery. There were too many, of this she was sure.

A smell of woodsmoke drifted over the porch and a faint haze hung in the air, but Elizabeth could see no fire. Loggers, she thought, or hunters, on the other side of the forest. Fire could be dangerous this time of year, though some evenings, when the sun hung low and refused to set, the sky seemed made of it.

Sometimes, whether out of frustration or so as not to let her anger or sadness show, Elizabeth left them and went out alone. When she returned, they would say they had worried about her, and she felt guilty but saw only new hats and emptier bottles of pear brandy.

She couldn't remember who they all were. Uncle George, Aunt Katya, Cousin Anya. Some from her parents' side, others from Emil's, some those distant family members or friends whose provenance she had never really understood. With their strange black coats and impractical shoes, their stiffly formal manners, and their dialectal words with strange vowels and unexpected clusters of consonants, they all became one. Aunt George, Uncle Katya, Cousin Chatchka. *Gruskovtort, bernspirog, kolak na pera.* Was it possible there were so many different names for a pear tart?

She stepped down from the porch onto the dry grass. It would scratch her feet, she knew, were she to take her shoes off, or her skin if she lay down like a dog and rolled in it, indulged in its rough caress. But then they would come for her, and help her back up, and tell her they worried, and she didn't want that. She took another step out and saw her shadow stretch to a vanishing point miles ahead of her. The sky wouldn't catch fire this evening, despite the smoke.

Some of them she swore she had never seen before: a strange pair of women, a lonely young man, an older one who wore a frock coat and shaded glasses. These came and went, never asking anything of her, not paying her any attention at all.

Emil had fixed that porch step. The heads of the nails he had hammered still shone, beginning to burnish after what, a year? Two? She had lost track of the time. He had never done anything like that, usually lost in his papers and books, but had made a job of it that one time, at least, sanded and planed the rough wood, held a spirit level so no one would stumble.

She unbuckled her shoes and let herself feel the brief scratch of the grass, then the dust, then the still-cool earth below. She pushed down, and the world pushed back at her.

The visitors had all arrived together, in a moment, and she wondered how they had managed, and supposed they had all walked from the village, as there had been sign of neither horse nor carriage. It was good they had come now, at the tip of the seasons, before the rain started and the road turned to mud, impassable until winter when frost hardened the ruts and snow smoothed the way for a sledge, good they had come at the end of summer when there was still warmth in the air, when the light held, when she could go walking.

It was time now. She put her shoes back on and stepped out for the forest.

She didn't want them around, not all the time, not even much of it. She wanted to feel grateful for their help but more often felt responsible for them, even though they mostly ignored her. She had quickly grown to like the quiet ones most, the ones who hardly looked at her and stood on the stairs or in the corners, the young man and the woman in the long, old-fashioned skirt who she thought must be distant cousins, and who sat at the edge of the grass for hours, sometimes, just near where she was passing now, though there was no sign of them today.

As she got closer, she felt the breath of the forest. Moss and mushroom, the dampness of the pre-ghost of frost, a curled tongue of yet-invisible mist reaching to her, something on the turn, beginning to rot. The heaving sadness of the late summer, its imminent end, roiled within her. She had always felt the sadness in everything, Emil told her that, even a sunflower, he said, handing her a bunch from the field on the other side of the village. They're the most purely joyous things I can think of, he'd said, and I know that you will find the sadness in them.

It was true, she had known it then and felt guilty again, at fault, as though she and she alone were responsible for the sadness in everything, and she had tried to believe that it wasn't her but that everything held its own sadness regardless of whether she perceived it or not. Her attempts had mostly been futile. Even Emil became exasperated. The sadness was in her, and not in the things around her.

But not now, though, now it felt different: the breath of the woods, that first touch of cold, preserved or premonitory, fat blackberries in the bramble, all brought . . . not *joy*, no, not that, but something else, she didn't know what, couldn't find the word or even identify the feeling. She was glad the visitors had come, and glad she had left them behind now. She was glad she had come out walking. Contentedness, perhaps, nothing more than that. As a girl, the bare sight of new-polished shoes and their warning of the return to school trawled her soul, but now the promise of the cool weight of the pear in her hand, one of those they had saved, its first bite against her teeth, the first chestnuts, woodfires, the languid air, and long dry grass drew her into the future.

And there had been no more school, not for a long time. If they had had children, perhaps, the ritual would have been repeated, and she would have felt pleasure in sending a son or daughter off with a clean apron and a sharp pencil, but that hadn't happened, and perhaps it had been for the best after all. Would the visitors leave when school began? Did they not have families of their own to care for? Jobs, earnings, houses to keep? Taxes to worry about and accounts to be settled? How long would they stay? They had been kind, yes, but she wanted them to leave now, they had only come to help, after she had let Lily go, there wasn't enough work for her, and, after Emil, there wasn't enough money either, she didn't need help, she said, and Lily had gone, and then the visitors had come, some time after that, some time after she hadn't had long enough time to be alone in the empty house.

She had almost reached the end of the grass now. It grew longer and thicker here, a different type, Emil would have known which, or pretended to know, at least. It had grown wild over the summer and now stood thick enough for mice to nest in. Emil had once had a vision, he'd told her like he sometimes did, or perhaps it was a dream, she couldn't remember now, of a man walking into the forest. That was it, that was all, nothing more. A man walking into the forest. He had written about it, like he often did, and even tried to paint it, though he hadn't been good with paint. Just that, only that. A man walking into the forest. It sounded like the beginning of an old story, she'd said, or a joke, "a man walked into the forest," but couldn't think what sort of story or joke it would be. Probably not much of one. She hadn't seen the painting for so long, and wondered what had happened to it. The visitors might have moved it or stored it away somewhere, she thought, the attic or the cellar where she never went, or even sold it for good money and the upkeep of the house now that she was alone. The thought gave her the sadness again, or perhaps it wasn't the thought that caused it; sometimes it just came on her, the sadness, tugged at her gut and ran through her veins, over her skin, like a wind that came from nowhere, a cold gust through the warmth, no reason, no cause, no motive.

The visitors brought no sadness with them, she told herself, they had come to help, to stop the sadness, and this was a good thing, but even as she told herself this, she thought of the twin sisters, and the young woman always alone with a book, and the quiet man with the beard, and she thought how their melancholy was palpable and made *her* want to help *them*, but she could not, because she could not reach them.

The grass grew thicker, the smell of the forest stronger. She stood at its edge now. She needed someone to invite her in. The woodsmen from the other side, perhaps, one of them might be passing through, or a friendly animal, a rabbit, or fox, like in a children's tale. Deep inside, the dark thickened, but there was still light enough for her to see a slip of a figure appear, then disappear among the trees. A second, only. Then again. There it was, a girl, a young one, Elizabeth thought. A flicker, little more, a flash. Again, the figure appeared, her back turned, then went again, deeper into the forest. A fleck of white in the deep green. Elizabeth thought she could hear a voice. This was enough. An invitation. Someone was there. Never alone.

Once inside, Elizabeth felt herself as if at the bottom of the sea, moving slowly across thick sand like some ancient pincered creature, barnacled and lugubrious, looking up at the canopy of leaves as if it were the surface of the water, filtering weak shafts of the late sunlight, dappling everything. The canopy shifted and waved so gently it was scarcely perceptible, whispering like the sea she had once seen at Ventspils or the sound of a thousand hushed voices. She moved slowly at first, big, heavy steps, picking her feet up deliberately for fear she should take leaves with her, but soon the path firmed up and opened out, the well-trodden route she had taken so many times before, but never alone. The forest's breath had been colder than the forest itself, and she relaxed into the warmth of the surroundings, the thickets to each side and the canopy above storing up the late summer heat. A thick silence wrapped around her like the heat, and she liked it. The loam underfoot found her steps and returned her quiet strength, and she liked it. She paused to watch birds—Emil would have known which ones—hop between branches, and she liked them and called to them and, even if they did not reply, was sure they were listening to her, too.

That was what she should do: listen to the forest, listen to what it could tell her. She paused, and looked for a place to sit, but no convenient log or stump proffered itself. It mattered not, she would just stand as still as she could, play statues, and listen.

She listened to the silence grow thicker and deeper, and then within that silence she began to discern patterns and figures, the path of the breeze, the fall of the heat, almost of the very light itself. The forest was alive with whispers and murmurs, echoes and traces. If she stood there long enough, she thought, she would surely learn to decipher them all, to be able to hear the forest speaking to itself.

As the sounds grew, the light faded, and shadows took on body. The visitors had come with her, she thought, some of them, at least. It was kind of them to come, but she did not want them now. They were only there to help, to share her company, for companionship, now that she found herself alone in the forest, but she had no need of them and they faded again, growing silent and indistinct as they headed back down the path or merged into the trees. One lingered, a young girl Elizabeth had known many years ago but whose name she could not quite remember. The girl had been a schoolmate but had gone missing, and no one knew what had happened to her, and no one ever spoke of her again. Elizabeth tried again to remember the girl's name, but as soon as she did, the girl had gone. It didn't matter, she thought, the girl would come back, would visit again, in some form or another. Nothing, no one, ever vanished completely. The heat of the summer was not leaving, or even fading, merely turning into something else: it became the colour of the leaves, the plump berries, the skins of the pears, the prickles of the beechmast, the thick bark of the trees, it became the rot that broke things down into the earth before reforming them as plant, or earth, or some other form of life. Everything left its trace, everything *was* trace. All energy was heat, and only when heat had finally gone would the visitors go, too, and that was a long way off.

That girl, she wasn't the only one, Elizabeth realised, there had been others, several people who had appeared in her life for a brief time, and then gone again, without warning or explanation. A man with big teeth who had said he was a friend of her father, a dark-skinned girl she had played with as though she were a sister, a man called Gilbert with a foreign accent. Little wonder she couldn't remember who all of the visitors were; there had been so many.

Night should be coming by now, but it was taking its time. The long evening light held, even this far into the forest. She should head back soon, but the path went on, its dirt and sand and stones well-worn, grass and bushes cleared to its edges, offering her a way through. She remembered the times she had passed this way before but could not remember who she had come with. Sometimes, the strange shapes the branches formed or the cawing of birds she couldn't name had spooked her, but now she felt only friendship being offered. Everything was whispering, and it was whispering to her. The light through the leaves spelled out words, but she couldn't read them. The trees wanted to speak to her. The trees had something to say.

She stopped. This couldn't be right. She felt scared a moment, and gathered herself. The trees were not speaking. Trees could not speak. She had come out for an evening walk only to be alone for a while, nothing more. The forest was the forest, the trees the trees, and the birds the birds. Nothing more. Everything had its place, and everything was in its place.

Emil had told her that moths were messengers from the dead and carried messages inscribed on their wings, but that we were not able to read them. He wasn't serious, it had been something he had read, but he had loved the idea. The moths had caused the blight on the pear trees.

But if the tree *had* spoken, if Elizabeth had let it speak, what would it have said to her?

There had always been someone at the bottom of the garden, in the long grass, at the edge of the woods, as long as she could remember. There she was again, just ahead, just slipping from view.

That one time Elizabeth had seen the sea, it had been for her. The space, the open, the endless vastness, the huge moil and roar of the waves, the salt wind stinging her face. The air had reached deep into her lungs and buoyed her up, though she was scared even to put her feet into the water. It had always been so: she was for the sea, the hills, the fields, for the wide-open spaces. The sea offered emptiness, loss, vastness; the forest held tiny loops and eddies, pockets and lapses, folds and creases. Little mysteries gathered at the foot of each tree, each turn of the path. The forest was not her, but she was welcome nevertheless. Even though she had walked this way before, the forest always showed itself anew, and always hid something else, a new warp or weft, another fork or turning. By the sea, or on the hills, time vanished; in the forest, time turned in on itself, reiterating itself constantly, the familiar ever unknown.

The trees hadn't spoken to her, but the birds were calling to her. Soon, she felt she would be able to understand the messages inscribed on the moths' wings. Time was all. The sea and the forest had different times, they were not of the human. Some of the butterflies in here lived only for a few days; some of the trees for a thousand years. She was merely passing through. If she listened carefully enough, if she could slow or speed up, everything would become clear. Emil would know that now: where he had gone, there was no more time. It had been the blight on the trees that had disturbed him so, sent him off down that final pathway. It had gone now, the strange white dusty fungus, cleared up as mysteriously as it had come, but only after Emil had left. He had taken it upon himself, and taken it with him. She would say that the next time she wrote to him. She still wrote him little postcards sometimes, simple messages, nothing more. She hadn't written since the visitors had arrived. She could tell him about them. She wrote but had nowhere to send her letters, because there was no address for where he was now.

She paused to take her shoes off, to rub her feet, and felt for the first time closed in, especially now the light was beginning to fail. She closed her eyes and breathed deeply, and she was back at the sea again. He had come to find her there, in her memory, in the story she told herself; she had been standing there on the shore and he had come there. She had seen him coming, or perhaps he had touched her shoulder and she had turned and seen him again, and they had cried, she thought, both of them. It had been such a long journey. "I came to find you," he had said, and she had begun to cry. She had travelled so far, all alone, and he had followed her and found her. I'm sorry, she had wanted to say, though was not sure if she ever did. She should write this to him, the next time she wrote. She should write that she was sorry. She was sorry that the blight had come and killed so many trees. She was sorry about the child, the baby that never was. She sat on the edge of a log—the woodsmen must have passed this way— and hoped and hoped and forced herself to hope that she would see him again, following her, that she would feel his touch again on her shoulder and turn and find him there. But not this time. There was no one behind her, only someone ahead of her. There she was again, the figure in the trees ahead of her. There she was: a young girl, running off to play German Jumps or Dead Johann. Not at the sea. There she had been afraid to put her feet in, but the forest was beckoning, welcoming. She would go on.

It wasn't she who had left, she thought, it had been him, in his way. He had started not being well, and she hadn't been either, so she'd taken the train, through all kinds of places, places she didn't know and had never heard of, and travelled until she could no more, until she'd reached the end, until the sea had stopped her, though she had heard there was an island out there, and she thought maybe she should try to reach the island, but no, the sea had been enough, it had been there that she had been lifted by the sea's open expanse. There was no time there, on that shore, by that sea. Not until he had come and she had seen him from afar or he had touched her shoulder, and then time had started again, and she had been back in the turmoil of the world, of life itself.

But it was good he had come, he had come so far to find her. They had had to separate. No one had done any wrong, but they could no longer stay together, not after that loss, because all they could see in each other, all they knew now of each other, was that pain. They had to leave, to be apart so each could start again, so each of them could have no past. He had been the first visitor, come to find her and to help her, or she had been, a visitor for him, no need for the messages of trees or leaves or moths' wings.

She got up again and followed the path. Somewhere ahead was a clearing where the light would still be there. That was where the figure had gone, the girl she knew to be herself when she was younger.

She could still write the letters, perhaps, but in a different way. She could write them by placing stones carefully, by collecting leaves or arranging twigs and branches in a particular form. She could write the words and leave them here, perhaps, in the forest, or by the lake where they would slowly fade and become one with the soil and water again. This was the best way to write to him, to anyone. What more would she need? Look at the tree, for example, this one here, right in front of her now. What did it need? Air, water, light. Of the human world, it cared little; it would be there if she were or not. The trees cared nothing of the human world until the woodsmen or the loggers came, or the fire that they had started. Nothing was far from the touch of the human. Nothing was an island; everything was everything else. The forest had once covered the entire country, she'd read, the whole continent, even, and now it was lost, lonely, going, dwindling, remembering what it had once been. Maybe the forest was sad for its own loss, she thought, then dismissed the idea. The forest knew nothing. The forest was ignorant of the tales told about it. The forest just was.

She listened again to the music it made: the creaks and hums, how they formed a harmony, a rhythm with the calls of the birds, the whispers of the animals, her own footsteps. The sounds grew until she could hear it all, each note perfectly placed in space and time. Was the forest making its music, or was it only in her hearing of it? Why should there be patterns? Why should there be form?

And did her life have form? Had she wanted that? Shape, order, logic, reason. What had she wanted? The past had become stronger than the future, it had amassed like a wave, built up pressure like a wine bottle or pickle jar ready to explode. Only it hadn't exploded, it had broken like a wave or dissipated like a cloud that had threatened storm and then passed without breaking. The visitors had come. Some of them were following her out here now, she was sure of it, even though she couldn't see them. It was like the ribbon of the typewriter, or a spool of thread now bare, though it had created something in exhausting itself. Elizabeth felt the weight of memory greater than the weight of anticipation. Now there was nothing to wait for, or to hope for. There was the light, the evening, the forest, and this was enough for her. She could look back, right now, but she didn't. She walked on.

It hadn't been the lack of the child that had taken him, nor his own writings, which he thought had come to nothing, nor the fall he had taken, nor the blight on the trees. There had been so much more to him than all that. It had been, she knew, the more general murk and tangle of his mind that had never been quite right. But she had been more. Her husband's life had not defined her. "Art is all we have," Emil had said. And even when he said it, Elizabeth had known that it might not be enough.

She always wanted to find a life in the world of things; Emil in the world of forms. A nice line, but not true, perhaps. Object and essence were indistinguishable, she knew that now, walking through the forest. Emil had never known that and had wanted to *make* sense of the chaos of life, and not *find* sense in that chaos. He had to work hard to do that. And herself? She had never borne children, raised a family; had she known life? Love was all they had, and that might not have been enough.

And this, this walk, this moment now, she could only do this by walking away from all that. Though again, turning back, turning a corner, she didn't know if she was walking away or walking *into*. This forest had unmade her, unmoored her. Here, now, she was coming to a space she was sure she had passed through a hundred times, yet each time it was the first.

One of the visitors, Elizabeth wasn't sure who, a sombre-looking young woman, appeared beside her and began to tell her a story. "I had a dream," she began, "and in this dream there was a house with two rooms and two rooms only. In one I lay asleep in the most comfortable bed, covered in soft, thick blankets. I slept so deeply and so soundly, yet I knew I was sleeping and felt myself more content than I could ever imagine. The other room was empty, save for a noose and the sound of it tightening. When I woke up from the dream, I realised that these were the two chambers of my heart."

The woman fell back into the trees, and Elizabeth sat herself down again on the stump of a tree. She knew where she was now, had been here before. A space opened, a hole in the forest. Up above, the canopy cleared to let in the sky, which had held its light, even this late. No shadows were cast. Everything was still. In front of her was that strange tree they had always called the Blind Accordionist because of its odd shape, hunched, ageless, and ever regrowing. She thought it might speak to her for a moment, but it remained silent. Another visitor came and sat next to her instead.

"Dear friend," he said, "you cannot cross here." And when she turned to look at him he had gone, and she didn't know who he had been, or if what he had told her was true. She stayed where she was and at the same time saw herself get up and leave, and cross the clearing and go back into the forest. She heard herself behind herself, still walking. She was the little girl collecting acorn cups and husks of beechmast, singing rhymes and playing skipping games, and the young woman writing in her diary, telling of how her father had died and her mother fallen ill, and the older one who would meet Emil and then leave him and then return. She was the young girl who had set one mirror opposite another to see herself reflected infinitely, and who had been told she would bring spirits into the world if she did so, and the woman who had watched as they had covered those same mirrors with black cloths when her husband died, and the woman who had removed the cloths, because she wanted to trap his spirit as it flew from this world.

And then she was one again, and whole again, and walking

again. She had been here before and would be here again. A vertigo of possibility overtook her, the fertile chaos of this life. She shivered with the forest itself as the breeze rose, her skin one with the air and the wind, each beat of her heart a footstep, each footstep a breath. Time became her and ceased to exist. Life was so fragile, and utterly inextinguishable. She had been, was, would be again, there to name the names of the unseen, untouched, unheard, unremembered, and transfigure them into and out of time. Those things that had been lost, or never happened at all, she would hold them. No, it was not time yet, she could not cross, she would need the names of things, to echo them, to sound them out, bring them back or conjure them into existence. She should try, yes, she thought, with his name, with the names she had called him, to his face and in secret, the breaths over his face while he slept and in his last illness, as if that would bring him back, how he had been and not what he became, from wherever he was now, and not just him, but the others, she would remember, and remember too what had *not* happened, remember what had never been seen.

She had always thought someone was following her when she came into the forest, and now knew it was herself, pulled by the mortal and touched by the ineffable, all her selves. They were all there, she could have them all, she knew as the visitors came again, behind her, and all of a sudden she remembered them, and knew who they all were, each and every one, and she remembered laughing with them, and laughed again. I am blessed to have had such, she thought as she walked on, and again they slowly dwindled as they spoke to her. "You're tired, aren't you?" they asked, and she was, but she wouldn't stop, not now, she was nearly there. The path went on, as far as the sea, perhaps, and the sea would wait for her, and the sea would be warm and invite her in, and she could hold the taste of a pear and feel its weight in her hand and the touch of his skin and the sound of his name and all the others, and she was leaving for an adventure, back through the forest, full and still, where she could hear the trees and their leaves and the birds in them and the animals under them and the light itself, and she was coming home now, and it wasn't art, it was love, and maybe maybe maybe it would, this time, be enough.

AFTERWORD
A GUIDE TO GUYAVITCH'S
NINE STORIES

LET ME BEGIN by saying that I have long been concerned with the question of beginnings. Where, for example, would be the right place for an essay such as this to open? Or—to consider the matter at hand more carefully—which among the chain of unpredictable yet inevitable events that form a tale would be the one for a story to alight on, and commence its narration? What is it that sets such events or thoughts into their motion?

The breathless sighting of sails in the offing, if not the docking of the ship in the port itself, will always make a fine opening. The rush to the harbour or the faces of the disembarkers as they glimpse this new land for the first time, or cast a cold eye upon the city to which they are returning. The arrival of a train in a station, large or small, our focus on either those arriving or those waiting. The shrill ring of the alarm clock would be another possibility, the groggy hand reaching out to silence it, the rapid cut to the brewing of coffee. The chance encounter (in a bar, bookshop, or theatre) of two strangers, destined to become lovers. The unexpected arrival of an unsigned letter, perhaps. The discovery of a body, of course, a quick section with the dog walker or jogger finding something unpleasant in the bushes, then cut to the hard-bitten cop shaking off their hangover and having to explain something to their rookie partner while quizzing the shaken discoverer. Someone walking across a field at dawn, the dew on their boots, the mist lifting with the rising of the sun—they're whistling a tune, I think, as they hop over a gate. Perhaps they have an eager dog bounding around their legs. Neither knows yet what the day holds, but there is anticipation, expectation, desire written into it. The hanging of the gun on the wall, unnoticed yet already loaded, a casual detail, a day like any other, its cargo signalled yet not announced.

Departure is always a promising start: the train building up a head of steam, or its electronic bleeping telling us the doors are about to close, the rush to the ticket barrier or the wait as the leaver gazes out of the window looking back on what now lies behind them, but we should consider, too, the false ending as beginning, the beginning that plays on the knowledge that much has already been done: let's get the band back together; the old-timer blackmailed into one last heist; the arrival of the mysterious stranger in town that a single person recognises. Beginnings never start at the beginning. Something has always already happened. The place we choose to start is but one moment in a constellation of many.

Notes such as these, for example, may be expected to give the "backstory." I dislike the term "backstory," for there is no backstory, no simple explanation or expurgation, neither apology nor apologia. There is, however, always a shadow story, a story's inverse. That which is not told, but which is part of the tale or the account. The exploration of this (and, in turn, what you are reading right now) is what we could call "forensic literature." Investigation becomes speculation, an inevitable launch into fiction, to remember what never was.

The roll of the dice, the spin of the wheel, or the deal of a hand of cards is perhaps the cleanest opening there could be. Fate made manifest; the future as a whim. As has become my habit of late, I wonder about Maxim Guyavitch, and what he thought as he sat down to write the opening line of his earliest (known) story. And where was he, I wonder? In a gloomy study with a view of rooftops? A cramped bedroom, tangled sheets, clothes strewn on the floor? A café, filled with smoke and steam and chatter? Busy packing a suitcase, ready for yet another departure? The long description of lancinating chill in the story "The Card Players" leads me to think Guyavitch was a man well familiar with cold, and suffering from a lack of heat at the time, but I admit the equal possibility that it was the height of a stifling summer and he wrote to invoke the icy, the gelid, the crystalline.

There is always a temptation to read a writer's work very closely against their life, as if all writing were a form of autobiography, but Guyavitch never played cards once in his life. Of this, I am sure. "The Card Players" is not a story about games; it is about beginnings. It is a story about the power of chance, chance cast against destiny.

I do, however, believe that Guyavitch had watched many games take place, though I admit the possibility that several other things could have influenced this story, one of which may have been Nikolai Gogol's play *The Gamblers*. This is a play with a plot both ludicrously complex and fantastically simple, as unpredictable and inevitable as the best plots should be. Ikharev, an itinerant gambler, checks into a rundown hotel in a remote Russian town, where he runs into three other card players who immediately recognise him as one of their own, namely, a cheat. They get together with a plan to fleece Glov, a rich landowner, who is in town with his idiot son who also likes to play cards. It gets complicated after that, but ends up with Ikharev destitute, realising only too late that he had been the patsy all along.

I suspect, but cannot prove, that Guyavitch saw *The Gamblers*. The play is rarely performed, it doesn't work well on stage. It would have been much better written a short story—Gogol's forte, after all.[1] It's difficult to show a game of cards on a stage. Stories and pictures do it better. Of the former, there are strangely few;[2] of the latter, many.[3]

Every gallery should have a picture called *The Card Players*. The daddy of them all, the image that founded its own genre, is

---

1   "We all come out from under Gogol's overcoat," said Dostoevsky (allegedly).

2   In Joseph Roth's *Radeztky March*, Kovacs has "an unreasonable fear of cards," insisting on playing only dominoes, while Kafka's Hunger Artist complains about card players as they distract his audience, and Daniil Kharms wrote, "as for card players, I would have them executed."

3   There's a great Otto Dix one, a whole series by Cézanne, a good Georges de la Tour, the lesser-known but vital *Les joueurs de tric-trac* by the Le Nain brothers (c. 1650), and—possibly contemporaneous with Guyavitch— Frank Gascoigne Heath's 1909 *A Game of Cut-Throat Euchre*. Photographs, even—a fine August Sander from 1920, *Farmers Playing Cards*, could almost be an illustration for a Guyavitch story.

Caravaggio's 1594 *Card Players* or *Cardsharps*. It doesn't have a precise title, is sometimes given other names, but is commonly known in Italian as *I bari*. *Bari* would be best translated as "cheats," though this is still not a perfect translation, as *barare* implies something slightly different to the more common *imbrogliare* or *fregare*, which merely mean to "rip off." *Un baro* is someone slightly more elegant, someone who has charm and wit and skill, and is more than a mere huckster or conman. *Un baro* is an inveigler, someone with a mark who is an almost-willing participant in their own deception. A storyteller, perhaps.

It's fitting that there are several names for Caravaggio's painting, because there are several paintings. Some estimates put the number as high as fifty, though how many of these are by Caravaggio, no one is quite sure (probably only two, maybe three). Whether "from the workshop of" or outright forgeries, less importance was placed on authenticity or originality in those days, the minor addition to the established theme or the skill shown in executing the set image being far more valued. Today, perhaps, we pay too much attention to concepts of authenticity or originality.

It has been suggested that Caravaggio's picture was an illustration for one of Cervantes's *Novelas Ejemplares*, most probably the tale "Rinconete y Cortadillo" (due to its Neapolitan references—both Cervantes and Caravaggio spent some unhappy time in the city). Cervantes wrote this collection around the turn of the seventeenth century, following the first part of *Don Quixote*, and quite how Caravaggio is supposed to have been aware of them I do not know, as he died in 1610. There are twelve original *novelas*, all separate tales tangentially linked, but more than one version exists of a number of them, while others have had their authorship disputed. Some reappear in *Don Quixote* itself. Minor works by major writers are so often the more interesting ones. Or the major works of minor writers, perhaps. After all, who gets to decide?

Caravaggio's cardsharps are playing "zarro," a Persian game that had been banned a century earlier by Francesco Sforza, the Duke of Milan, for being socially dangerous.[4] Card games are, of course, socially dangerous, and as we have seen, can never end. The picture warns us of dangers while revelling in them, and it is for this paradoxical reason, perhaps, that every gallery should have a picture of card players, if not by Caravaggio, or Cézanne, or Sander, then at least by Cassius Coolidge.

Coolidge was born to strict Quaker parents in upstate New York in 1844, and after a series of failed endeavours (druggist, journalist, banker, playwright, cartoonist, and portrait photographer) took to painting. Despite his lack of training, his pictures have become some of the most well-known and valuable works of art of the modern era. In 1894, he painted *Poker Game*, and he followed this up ten years later with the first in the sequence that became known as *Dogs Playing Poker*.

Each of the sixteen pictures in the sequence are variations on the theme, much like that of Caravaggio, or Cervantes. The sequence, by which I mean the repetition of form with minor variants potentially having a major impact, is a structuring principle

---

4 Sixtus V, who may have been pope when the picture was painted, issued an edict against gambling but stopped short of banning the playing of cards outright, instead levying a hefty tax on card players. It has been suggested that a later pope coined the caveat, "Foolish the man who plays with five aces and no knife."

for much great art, from Petrarch's *Canzoniere* to Satie's *Gymnopédies* and *Gnossienes* to Cindy Sherman's *Untitled Film Stills*.

In 2015, *Poker Game* sold at Sotheby's for $658,000. Given the value of these pictures, it is little wonder that fakes abound, particularly as Coolidge seems to have been unconcerned about ownership of his work: copies, interpretations, spoofs, and outright rip-offs have conspired to flood the popular imaginarium. (It is possible that one of the definitions of the spurious category of "great art" is exactly its potential for generating copies, interpretations, spoofs, and outright rip-offs.) One of the series in particular catches my eye, a later work entitled *His Station and Four Aces*.

The picture features seven dogs (four players, two observers, and a conductor) in a train compartment, by night. The train is coming into a station (the lights on the platform and other canine passengers waiting to board can just be seen through a semi-raised window blind), the conductor is doing his rounds to announce this, and yet the boxer dog, seated to the left of the picture and one of its dual foci, holds four aces (an incredibly rare hand in human poker) and is aghast. His station has come; he will not be able to play his hand.[5]

The sequence with repetition of form and minor variants is much like a train, and the interior of a train, with its enclosed

---

5   The dreamlike eeriness of this picture recalls certain pictures of Paul Delvaux (I am thinking particularly of *Der Wachmann*, *Loneliness*, or *Forest Station*), as well as more thematic genre paintings, in which the genre isn't card players but the interiors of train carriages: Tirzah Garwood's *Train Journey*, Leopold Egg's *The Travelling Companions*, John Tenniel's railway guard peering at Alice through an oversized pair of binoculars, and a number of pictures from Max Ernst's sequence *Une semaine de bonté*, for example.

spaces, curious elongation and compression of time, and enforced yet accidental intimacy with strangers is (as the characters in "An Incident on the Train to Lvov" note) a perfect setting for a short story.[6] The train possesses dreamlike and sinister qualities, as does a good story. Even the most overcrowded, underfunded commuter services can have their touch of the oneiric, though I admit I may be stretching the point here.

Any regular train rider becomes a careful observer and keen fabulist. Guyavitch, I am certain, was a man who spent much time travelling third class himself. "An Incident on the Train to Lvov" is clear proof of this. I see him, sitting in the corner of a cramped compartment, pen in hand, listening carefully and attentively while simultaneously being a thousand miles distant. Guyavitch was a man who listened to everything, and listened well, I think.

Isaac Babel, too, spent a lot of time on trains. Though his *Odessa Stories* are a part with the place he was born and grew up in, a place he listened to carefully, felt viscerally, and recreated through his fiction, he only wrote them after he had left. He may have stayed in Odessa forever, if he hadn't been refused entry to the university (not due to academic failing, but because he was Jewish). So Babel (a man "who loved to confuse and mystify people," according to his daughter) headed to Kiev, then Saint

---

6   The curious reader is directed to Isaac Babel's "Salt," Bruno Schulz's "Sanatorium Under the Sign of the Hourglass," Sigizmund Krzhizhanovsky's "The Branch Line," Charles Dickens's "The Signal-Man," Primo Levi's "One Night," Georgi Gospodinov's "A Second Story," Italo Calvino's "The Adventure of a Traveler," Thomas Bernhard's "Early Train," Diego Marani's "The Man Who Missed Trains," Lydia Davis's "The Magic of the Train," Eley Williams's "Alight at the Next," Joanna Walsh's "Hauptbahnhof," and Clemens Meyer's "The Beach Railway's Last Run," among several others. Tolstoy died at a railway station.

Petersburg (which became Leningrad), then Romania (possibly), then Georgia, then had a spell back home before the army (the source of his *Red Cavalry* stories), then Poland, Ukraine, wherever he was posted. Finally, having become a recognised writer at a time when it may have been better to have stayed unrecognised, he went to Moscow. Babel's stories[7]—minimal and maximal, tender and brutal, clear eyed and woozily romantic, funny and bitter—earned him enough reputation to grant him the freedom of long stays in Paris, more trains, but less writing. In the 1930s, dangerous times for a truth-telling Jew, his output ceased almost entirely. "I have become a master of the genre of silence," he said.

Like Guyavitch's stories, Babel's stories have a constant longing for home, a home never to be found, as it no longer existed and could only be reconstructed through memory. It would be wrong to say such a man found his home in his stories, but parts of Odessa could be rebuilt using them as a plan.

We don't know where Guyavitch's home was[8]. How many of us truly know where home is? "Pilgrim Souls," like most of the *Nine Stories,* is about home, and its absence.

Villages which have moved and been rebuilt are many, those evacuated or abandoned even more. Few countries are without their eerie ruins, their ghost towns, environmental or hydroelectric plans gone awry, silenced disasters. Pripyat, near Chernobyl, is now one of Ukraine's biggest attractions, featuring on bucket lists for the adventurous traveller. Imber, a small village on Salis-

---

7 Here I think about how appropriate his name is, this man of many languag es: born into Yiddish and Hebrew, he wrote his first stories in French, later learning Russian, Ukrainian, and German.

8 There have been several claims made—see the section on suggested further reading for more information.

bury Plain in England, found itself in the middle of an arbitrarily decreed army testing range in 1943 and now only lets its aged inhabitants and their descendants visit once a year, a military *Brigadoon*. The town of Plymouth on the island of Montserrat lies under volcanic ash, a future Pompeii. In Kalyazin, Potosí, and Sant Romà de Sau, church spires rise from lake waters in spells of drought; in Shi Cheng, Capel Celyn, and Neversink, bells are said to be audible if you listen carefully enough, on the quietest of nights. Now villages, towns, and cities all across the world await fire or flood, and I wonder if Guyavitch's story is not one of aching nostalgia, but of foresight.

Bruno Schulz—another of Guyavitch's contemporaries—never left his hometown but lived in several different countries. He was born in 1892, just two years before Babel, in Drohobych, near Lvov. This was in Galicia, then part of the Austro-Hungarian Empire, which had been part of the Kingdom of Poland, but later found itself in the short-lived Western Ukrainian People's Republic, then the Second Polish Republic, then the Soviet Ukraine. His stories contain nothing of this, almost blissfully impervious to the changes around themselves, obsessively concentrating on his family and his hometown, a place that could also be built from the descriptions in *The Street of Crocodiles* and *Sanatorium Under the Sign of the Hourglass*, though if it were, it would seem no real place, but the dream of one, the town dreaming itself.

I wonder where, exactly, the passengers in "An Incident on the Train to Lvov" are, and where the city of N— is. I wonder if they pass through Drohobych, or if they are east of there, near Brody, where Joseph Roth was from.

While Babel may have had rootlessness forced upon him, and Schulz had it happen around him, Roth chose it. Born two years after Schulz and some two hundred kilometres east of him, young Joseph moved to Vienna when he was twenty, spent some time on the Eastern Front, saw his homeland collapse, then moved to Berlin, with spells in Poland, Italy, Russia, then finally, after leaving Germany in 1933, to Paris. "A man whose element was turbulence," wrote Michael Hofmann, one of Roth's translators. It would be wrong to call Roth a writer of short stories, but it would also be wrong to categorise him at all. He wrote journals, journalism, letters, feuilletons, novels, memoirs, fragments, all about loss and nostalgia and drinking and wandering. A man who had little time, I think, for any conventions and restrictions of genre.

That said, defining things can be hugely satisfying. The Periodic Table of the Elements: all physical matter classified and arranged. The International Phonetic Alphabet: each sound the human mouth is capable of producing given a symbol. The Beaufort Scale: something as intangible and powerful as the wind itself pinned down. Linnaean taxonomy: life, defined. Dictionaries, encyclopaedias, bibliographies, catalogues raisonnés. A train timetable: all that chaos and complexity neatly arranged into columns of places and times, destinations and arrivals.

Much of this classifying impulse, I believe, is at work in Gogol's clerks and low-level functionaries, Kafka's job as an insurance man, Babel's jobbing crooks and squaddies, Bruno Schulz's shopkeepers, cooks, and cleaners, Robert Walser's quiet dreaming of the functionary, the orderly, "little, but thoroughly."[9]

Guyavitch never had much time, and it is as if he knew this.

---

9 The motto of the Benjamenta Institute in Walser's *Jakob von Gunten*.

Guyavitch was a man, I feel, always looking for a home, but a home that did not exist. "The writer operates at a peculiar crossroads where time and place and eternity somehow meet. His problem is to find that location," wrote Flannery O'Connor, and this was very much Guyavitch's problem. I wonder if he ever did find that place. So little we know.

I have always wondered, for example, how this man who—I believe—moved so much carried his writings with him. Joseph Roth didn't bother, happy to lose them once published. I wonder if Guyavitch was the same. What did he carry? A notebook, or but a few scraps of paper? A typewriter seems unlikely. Pen or pencil? His apparent reluctance in this respect, his almost a priori refusal to be commemorated, may be one of the reasons so little is known of him.

According to W. G. Sebald, Robert Walser was another writer "only ever connected with the world in the most fleeting of ways." In his essay "Le promeneur solitaire," Sebald writes of Walser that "nowhere was he able to settle, never did he acquire the least thing by way of possessions. He had neither a house, nor any fixed abode, nor a single piece of furniture . . . Even among the tools a writer needs to carry out his craft were almost none he could call his own. He did not, I believe, even own the books that he had written."

In 1929, Walser voluntarily admitted himself to the Waldau mental hospital in Bern. Adolf Wölfli was there, too. Wölfli had been admitted thirty years previously, then a dangerously violent psychotic, but he had begun to draw, and his doctor, Walter Morgenthaler, took an interest in the work, giving Wölfli a new pencil and two large sheets of paper every Monday morning. By

Wednesday, the pencil would be used up, and Wölfli would beg scraps of paper from other inmates or find packing paper, tissues, or labels and use the stub of his pencil or anything else he could find to cover them with his incredibly intricate drawings. Each Christmas, he was given a box of coloured pencils. Over thousands and thousands of pages, and more than twenty years, Wölfli told and retold his life as an epic fantastical narrative, forty-five volumes of it, in which he projected himself as a knight, an emperor, and a saint.

Walser may have known Wölfli, though their stays only overlapped a year. Wölfli died in 1930. Over the next twenty-six years, Walser kept on writing, also using a pencil, in microscopic handwriting, his letters but a millimetre high, using an old-style Germanic script, *Sütterlinschrift*. He called these writings the *Bleistiftgebiet*, the "pencil zone." He used envelopes, newspapers, the backs of business cards, receipts, calendar pages, often torn into long strips and sometimes written on in two directions, filling the paper entirely. Thousands of them. They were only discovered after his death, and for a long time thought to be in code.[10]

While taxonomies offer their pleasures, however, they are usually wrong. Linnaean classification cannot always cope with our increased understanding of the natural world. The Periodic Table has had to be constantly reinvented. The Beaufort Scale

---

10 While in a Nazi insane asylum, Hans Fallada wrote some three books in microscopic handwriting, constantly rotating the page and writing between the lines until the paper seemed a sheer block of black, staying his possible execution while he wrote. In 1944, the Russian poet Tatiana Gnedich translated all of Byron's *Don Juan* (from memory, with improvements) onto a few sheets of paper, each letter smaller than a pin head, when imprisoned in a Soviet labour camp.

has no mention of a wind-battered heart, and the International Phonetic Alphabet has no symbol for a guttural roar or a cry of grief. While there is pleasure in attempting to put order on the random chaos of this world, I—like Guyavitch—have little time for taxonomies, or genres. When things become blurred, they become interesting.

Daniil Kharms, for example. Born in Saint Petersburg in 1905, Kharms wrote absurdist poems, brutal children's fables, minute-long plays, and five-line novels, often all at the same time. In his apartment, he kept a contraption made from rusty springs, empty cigarette packets, a bicycle wheel, and some jam jars. He said it was "a machine" and, when asked what kind, replied, "No kind. Just a machine." Kharms called his writings *sluchai*—a near-untranslatable word that can mean event, incident, opportunity, occasion, emergency, circumstance, or chance. He had no school or genre so formed his own movement, *Oberiu*.[11] It had one other member.[12]

In Kharms's world, old ladies invite themselves into your flat to die or develop a habit of falling out of windows, shattering into pieces as they hit the pavement. Pushkin is incapable of sitting on a chair and eventually has his legs replaced with wheels. Men in black coats appear at the moment of erotic climax, and people disappear without warning. Hunger, bad alcohol, and random violence inhabit cramped apartments. Stories end abruptly, often with a slap in the face to the reader, or an assertion that the writer can't be bothered anymore. His stories are grim jokes in which every line isn't a punch line as much as a punch. Kharms is Gogol

---

11 A name chosen, Kharms said, because it means nothing at all.
12 Kharms's friend Alexander Vvedensky.

starved to the bone, Kafka in a really bad mood. His stories are the things Babel's characters may have had nightmares about, or the hallucinations Robert Walser suffered. I wonder if Guyavitch ever read him.

"Jenny Greenteeth" has nothing to do with Kharms. It may have been inspired by a story about the mining town of Falun in southern Sweden, described as being "as horrible as hell itself" by Linnaeus when he visited in 1733. Falun had been a centre for copper mining since the tenth century, and income from the mines propped up Queen Christina's imperial ambitions and attempts to make Stockholm one of the several cities known as the "Athens of the North."[13] In letters written during his stay there, Linnaeus described the rickety wooden ladders descending hundreds of feet into the pits, the sweat pouring from the miners' bodies as though they were swimmers more than miners, the obligatory drunkenness (breakfast was three or four pints of ale), the bread made from a flour of tree bark. The town was divided into two sides, which became known as the "delightful side" and the "hellish side." The hellish side, the side of the mines, consisted of the Great Pit and the Great Mountain. Men dug in the pit or tunnelled under it and dragged out the biggest rocks they could haul. They heated the rocks to an extreme temperature, then smashed them open to extract the copper ore. This process gave off thick clouds of sulphur, leading the entire town (including the delightful side) to be frequently swathed in thick clouds of stinking murk. The pit was where they dug, the mountain made from what they discarded.

On Midsummer's Eve in 1687, the mine collapsed, making

13 Other contenders include Edinburgh, Vilnius, Liège, Jyväskylä, and Huddersfield.

the pit even deeper. In 1719, miners found a body in a disused and flooded tunnel. "Fat" Mats Israelsson had been perfectly preserved (perhaps by the high mineral content of the water in which he had drowned), and was identified by his former fiancée, Margaret Olsdotter, now an old woman, who had not seen him for over thirty years. Once in the open, the body turned to something approaching stone, leading him to be known as the "petrified miner." They buried him again, then dug him up again in 1860 when the floor of the church in which he had been buried began to subside and put him on display in a glass case until 1930.

Guyavitch may have heard this original story, or heard Achim von Arnim's ballad about it, or seen Hugo von Hofmannsthal's play on the subject, or read Johan Peter Hebel's brief tale "Last Farewell," or E.T.A. Hoffman's longer "The Mines of Falun." Hoffman's story was originally published in *The Serapion Brethren*, a four-volume collection of stories[14] that Hoffman originally attributed to various hands (some real, others fictional[15]) before eventually claiming sole responsibility. Why Hoffman would want to do this is unclear. Perhaps he merely wanted to evade the burden of authorship, the cruel glare of critical scrutiny.

While scopophobia is the fear of being looked at, eisoptrophobia the fear of seeing one's own reflection, and ommetaphobia is the fear of eyes, it seems strange that as yet, there is no word for the fear of being photographed. All of these conditions are, in some ways, connected to the fear of being photographed,

---

14 Not unlike Cervantes's *Novelas Ejemplares*.

15 These included Adelbert von Chamisso and Baron Friedrich de la Motte Fouqué. (For the latter, see *The Biographical Dictionary of Literary Failure*, entry no. 11)

but there is more, surely, something unique—is it the fear of discovery? Or the fear of seeing oneself in a past moment? Is it a more atavistic fear of exposure to the rays of the camera? Or of what ghosts the picture may reveal? How can you watch without being seen? Is this what "Sosia and the Captain" is about? Or is this yet another tale of shifting identities, rootlessness, dissimulation, and fear of exposure? Or is it, more simply, a love story?

"I photograph to find out what something will look like photographed," said Gary Winogrand, and Guyavitch wrote, I might say, to find out what things were like once he had written about them. That, however, would be to suppose that there are "things" that exist independently of our way of seeing them, or knowing them, and I am increasingly uncertain if this is true.[16] Telophobia is a fear of endings, or of explanations.

Of the story "Dead Johann," I have nothing to say.[17]

"Both in art and in our general ideas about the passage of human life there is assumed to be a general abiding *timeliness*," wrote Edward Said in his essay "Thoughts on Late Style." A life should adequately correspond to its allotted span, and art should respect that. But it doesn't work that way, does it? Said goes on to write that "artistic lateness" is not "harmony and resolution"

---

16 "We usually regard the word as the shadow of reality, its symbol," wrote Bruno Schulz. "The reverse of this statement would be more correct: reality is the shadow of the word."

17 It is, ironically, one of the most discussed of all the Guyavitch stories. The curious notion that the story is somehow "cursed" has been floated by some readers, possibly simply because it is excised from a number of editions of the stories, replaced with a blank page or erasure marks. That it is the key to all of Guyavitch's work, as some feverish commentators have suggested, is an interesting idea, but if so, I fear what may lie behind any door it would open.

but "intransigence, difficulty and contradiction," and for proof of this there is in the story "The Visitors" an example of Guyavitch's late style.[18]

We cannot even know this was the last story Guyavitch wrote, but I feel sure that it is. It has both a leaving of home and a homecoming, an end and its beginning. It is valedictory and welcoming. It has intransigence, difficulty, and contradiction and holds them all, smoothing nothing away. Again we are brought back to Guyavitch's choice of the short form. There is no destiny in a short story. It explains nothing. A novel ties everything up and turns life into fate. A story goes on, shifting, being told and retold. It has no home, it continues its wandering.

And yet: There has to be an ending. Books demand one, readers demand one, life demands one.

In February 1852, Gogol burnt all of his manuscripts after the Devil played a practical joke on him and told him to. He died a week later. Seventy-two years after that, it wasn't quite tuberculosis that finished Kafka, aged forty, in a sanatorium just outside Vienna, but its laryngeal form, which made eating almost impossible. While editing the final draft of "A Hunger Artist," he starved to death. Fifteen years after that, in May 1939, Joseph Roth died in "increasingly distressed circumstances" (according to the *New York Times* obituary), an impoverished alcoholic. Scarcely a week earlier, Isaac Babel had had a knock at the door in the night from the drivers of the one-way taxi to the Lubyanka. "They did not let me finish," were his last known words. (A series of stories about a small-time gangster

---

18 The ultimate "late style" being—as Babel has it—"the genre of silence."

who makes his way through the Soviet system went missing; in 1987, a KGB agent claimed he'd burned them.) It can never really be known, but Babel spent up to two years there, eventually being murdered in 1941, the year Daniil Kharms, in Leningrad under siege from Nazi forces, had a similar call and simulated insanity to at least get himself into a psychiatric ward. On February 5, 1942, his wife Marina Malich managed to scrape together enough food to take to her husband, and when she arrived at the hospital was told he had died of starvation three days earlier. Eight months later, Bruno Schulz, still in Drohobych, now under Nazi occupation, was walking back from the baker's, where he had almost miraculously managed to procure a loaf of bread. He was murdered by a shot from a Nazi officer who was the jealous rival of another Nazi officer who had not yet murdered Schulz but instead used him to paint pictures in his house. (Drawings, paintings, and a story called "The Messiah" went missing, and have never been found.) Fourteen years later, on Christmas Day, 1956, a group of children out walking discovered the body of Robert Walser lying in the snow. Walser, as was his custom, had also gone out walking. His hat had fallen off. The police took photographs, and now everyone can see the scene. Fifty years earlier, in the *Geschwister Tanner*, Walser's first book—the story of Simon Tanner, who likes to take solitary walks and has plentiful siblings—Simon is out alone in the snow and comes across a man lying in the road. The man's hat is across his face and he is wearing a yellow suit, too thin for the snow but similar to one Walser himself had worn when younger. "His face and hands had long since frozen," wrote Walser, "and his clothes clung to his frozen body." Simon pulls a "small, thin booklet" from the dead man's coat pocket. "It seemed to contain poems; Simon no longer distinguished the characters. It had become utter night. The stars sparkled through the gaps in the fir trees, and the moon was watching the scene in a narrow, delicate hoop."

I could say that what we do undoes us, and that what we make in turn makes us. I could write about how we tangle with the world and how the imaginary can become the real, but that would not be true. So often, it is nothing but the brutality and arrogance of others that destroys. These writers all live their afterlives in their work, or what we have of it. But so many have none. We don't know what happened to Guyavitch, so what can we do but invent him?

Endings are the most difficult, always. Perhaps we should trust middles, after all, the underrated muddle, the less told, the difficult part. If beginnings are never really quite what they seem, neither are endings. There's a difference between ending and stopping. How to end something. The tearful departure, the marriage announcement. The poignant moment as the protagonist heads off again, down the road or upstream, wondering what may next befall them. The pack is shuffled again, the clock reset. The neat tie-up, the sudden reveal, the twist. The epiphany, perhaps, or the suspended moment. The gradual fade or the sudden

SUGGESTIONS FOR
FURTHER READING

THE WORLD OF Guyavitch studies is large, often obscure, and mostly perplexing. Listed here are but a few of the books and essays that, I hope, the reader may find of use or interest. To present a full catalogue would be an impossible, inexhaustible task, but know that the work is out there, waiting for you, when it is time.

Reading Guyavitch: A Critical Introduction, Jean Lefevre and Jeanne Lefebvre, eds. (Agloe University Press, 1978)

There is a corpus of critical literature on Guyavitch, a body of work that abounds in prepositions and hesitations. This collection contains a number of such essays: Weissbrot's "Towards a Hermeneutics of Doubt: The Cases of Felisberto Hernández and Maxim Guyavitch," Whitbread's "An Approach to the Unapproachable: Reading Kafka through Guyavitch," and Panebianco's "Against Certainty: Guyavitch and Krzhizhanovsky." As well as these, this book contains Freudian, Lacanian, Foucauldian, Derridean, Deleuzian, Kristevan, and Barthesian readings of the stories. Not recommended for the general reader.

(Once, and only once, I was invited to attend the annual conference of the Guyavitch Society. When I arrived at the designated location, I found nothing but a crumpled cigarette packet and two empty bottles of Zapovit. Since that day, I have heard nothing more of or from the Society, and cannot be sure they exist any longer.)

The Nine Chairs, Bernd Holer (Molloy & Malone, 1956)

Although Guyavitch is never mentioned in this slim, allusive, enigmatic, and elegiac novel, I am certain it is based on him. The unnamed main character sits in a room empty save for the titular chairs, reflecting on his slim, allusive, enigmatic, and elegiac life.

A Cartography of Loss: My Search for Guyavitch's Places, Lilian Mountweazel (Argleton Press, 2009)

There are some few dedicated pilgrims who have spent their lives trying to locate the villages or towns in which they believe Guyavitch's stories to be set. It's Plovdiv, they say, or Cluj, or Drohobych. It's in Galicia, Moravia, Transdniestria.

A Cartography of Loss is the story of one woman's quest to find these places, rendered interesting only by her utter refusal to acknowledge an important truth: the places she is looking for do not exist.

Guyavitch's stories, surely, aren't based in any particular village or town, but an amalgam of places, a superimposition of one upon another. Mountwealze, however, does accept this.

This book reminds me of another title, which I shall not name, by a reasonably well-known mid-twentieth-century writer who claimed to have a great friendship with a much-better-known mid-twentieth-century writer. The book she wrote about this friendship is fascinating, but mostly because it fairly rapidly becomes clear to the reader that she hardly knew him at all, that their "friendship" was almost entirely wishful thinking on her part. It's the lack of self-awareness that makes this supposed memoir become a classic of unreliable narration.

As Mountwealze travels from Leipzig to Brno, from Sarajevo to Kraków, from Lvov to Odessa, she tells us more about her own life (which is, in truth, dull) than about Guyavitch, about whom she seems to know very little.

Reisen mit einer magischen Lanterne: eine Geheimnisse des deutschen Kinos, Katerina Brac (Exit Verlag, 1967)

To say that Guyavitch's work has cinematic qualities is axiomatic; that the stories have never been filmed is baffling. This memoir tells the story of how it was once, at least, attempted.

Brac (a poet herself) claims to be a distant relation to Ana Brac, a filmmaker who worked in Germany in the early 1900s. "My great-aunt first appears," Brac writes, "as if by magic, at the beginning of a century, riding the endless flat countryside, from one *Kinotopp* to another, country fairs or village halls, Denmark to Poland, carrying magic lanterns and shadow puppets, fat wax candles and lightbulbs as delicate as soap bubbles, each one a miracle in itself. Flying horses, glass palaces, sea monsters, and princesses all carefully folded into a valise. She carried flickers and fades, wonders in a travelling bag. She would show children how she worked such magic, enchanting and enlightening them at the same time. Soon men would come with their Bioscopes and Vitascopes, dismissing tricks for ignorant peasants, promising life itself projected onto the bare white walls or starched sheets.

"Sometimes," Brac continues, "my great-aunt would close herself away and watch nothing but the movement of shadows on the sides of the tent, or gaze at the quality of the light itself. She had the power to enchant herself as much as others."

And then, she goes on, there was a relationship. One of her colleagues, perhaps; we know so little (and much of Brac's account is pure speculation). There is a move to Berlin, or a town just outside, where a new city is being built: Babelsberg. The mountain of babble, of languages, their own holy wood.

She makes films, perhaps appears in them herself. Her name appears on one-reelers ranging from low-rent rip-offs (*Lupin Arsène Meets Herlock Sholmes*) to high-concept schlock horror (*The Nights of Pierre Andrézel*), a whole sequence of comedies and tragedies involving gamblers, stolen paintings, train crashes, mysterious doubles, apparitions.

At some point around this time, the reader can intuit, Brac must have read the Guyavitch stories, or perhaps even known the man himself. She draws a group of people around her, two men (Max and Jules) and two women (Maria and Olga) and they drive north. Their journey to the Baltic coast and the summer they spent filming there (an inordinate amount of time, given that most films of this period were knocked out in an afternoon) is described at length. At a certain point, Maria and Olga both leave. The wind became too much for them.

Brac finds an archive that notes that a film titled *Grünezähne* and bearing her great-aunt's name, running to an hour in length (rare in that period), was shown in a number of cinemas in the early 1920s, but no copies survive. (Silver nitrate, so fickle.)

And what I wonder, on reading this book, is not what happened to this film of the story "Jenny Greenteeth," but if Brac may have been influential in its composition. Perhaps it was not a film of the story, but perhaps the story is of the film.

"Notes on the Whimsical," David Kingston (unpublished)

Guyavitch's writing has sometimes been dismissed as "merely whimsical." Needless to say, I do not hold with this opinion. That said, however, this essay (which came into my hands via the author himself[1]) caused me to rethink. Kingston begins with Susan Sontag's observation in "Notes on 'Camp'" that "many things in the world have not been named; and many things, even if they have been named, have never been described," then makes a claim that the Whimsical is, or should be, a critical category, an aesthetic, a tradition, a field all of its own, standing alongside the Gothic, the Pastoral, and the Classical. "The Whimsical," he continues, "is the realm of provincial art galleries, random museums (pens, pencils, straw, salt), waking dreams, Sunday afternoons, late October, villages or regions but not cities or nations."

We do not, sadly, have space here for the whole essay, but I will quote selectively below:

---

[1]   "I was going to throw this in the bin," he told me, "but thought that you might be interested in it."

While pareidolia—as long as it's not sinister—is often Whimsical, and anthropomorphism usually is, things like pictures of dogs playing cards are definitely not Whimsical. This is partly due to their ubiquity. The Whimsical is always liminal, half-remembered, half-imagined, even as it is taking place.

Walter Benjamin on Robert Walser's stories: "If we were to attempt to sum up in a single phrase the delightful yet also uncanny element in them, we would have to say: they have all been healed." There is no better definition of the Whimsical.

Natalie Babel said her father's stories do "not differentiate between important and trivial details." This could be seen as a characteristic of the Whimsical.

The Whimsical is neither masculine nor feminine. Such categories are so tiresome, after all, and so arbitrary, so inadequate. The Whimsical resists the macho. In its list-making and collecting, its love of detail, its pleasure in the intricate, the small-scale, the miniature; if it is masculine, then it is the masculinity of the garden shed. This may be the Whimsical's most important contribution.

Ulysses is whimsical: lists, questions, minutiae.

In the realm of the Whimsical, death is just one more thing that might happen.

Things in life can seem Romantic, or Fantastic, or Surreal. So little of life is Whimsical, and this perhaps, is life's tragedy.

The Whimsical: funny about serious things; serious about funny things.

There is the tiny, and there is the vast. There is the subatomic order of things, and the universal, eternal, beyond comprehension. Much that lies in between these two things is dull, or inexplicable, or mundane. The Whimsical is the first of these two things, but always has a tacit understanding, knowledge, or awareness of the latter.

Realism reduces the universal to a human scale; the Whimsical makes it smaller.

The qualities of lightness and quickness as described by Italo Calvino in *Six Memos for the Next Millennium* are key elements of the Whimsical.

"The tone does not suit the subject: it detracts from the serious message"—a common criticism of the (mis-understood) Whimsical.

The Whimsical is *never* ironic, though our enjoyment of it may be.

An incomplete list of the Whimsical:

Black light theatre; Brian Eno's Obscure Records (1975–1978); Bruegel (the elder); Burano; Cassiano dal Pozzo's Paper Museum; clocks (water, cuckoo, grandfather, alarm, whatever—all clocks, any clocks); Daniil Kharms; dioramas; Edmund Dulac; Edward Gorey; Edward Lear; Erik Satie; expressionism; footnotes; Georges Perec; hockets; Ivor Cutler; Jacques Tati; Jan Švankmajer; Jaromir Hladík; Jill McDonald's illustrations for Puffin Books; Joseph Cornell; Juan Muñoz; Kafka's "Kübelreiter"; Kleist's essay "The Puppet Theatre"; Yayoi Kusama; Lewis Carroll; lighthouses; lists; Lotte Reiniger; Marc Chagall; Marcel Schwob's life (but not his work); marionettes; metronomes; Moon Wiring Club; *Zazie dans le Métro* (book *and* film); mime (but Lecoq, not Marceau); midafternoons; the mise en abyme; Nabokov (but *Pnin*, not *Pale Fire*); Nikolai Leskov; Yuri Norstein; Oliver Postgate; Ana Maria Pacheco; 'pataphysics; Paul Klee; penny-in-the-slot automata; pillow books; Portmeirion; Richard Brautigan; Edith Rimmington; Rie Nakajima; short stories with long titles; small things that should be large; large things that should be small; stop-motion animation; the bass clarinet; the glockenspiel; the celeste, the harmonium (but not the harpsichord); E-flat minor; a trio or quintet, but not a quartet; the sound of a musical box, but rarely the object itself; the last ten minutes of *8 ½*; the Brothers Quay; *The Tempest*; the train scene from *Spirited Away*; umbrellas; *Valerie and Her Week of Wonders*; windmills; *Wunderkammern*.

I have an acquaintance at a university that has a chair of both Pseudo and Crypto Bibliography,[2] and thought that the essay might interest her. I sent her a copy, and she replied, somewhat brusquely, I feel: "Meretricious persiflage. Do not bother with this unless you want to sabotage what little semblance of a career you already have."

Maxim Guyavitch: A Life, Alfred Huggenberger (Thomson & Thompson, 1978)

Maxim Guyavitch: A Life, Johannes Jegerlehner (Dupond and Dupont, 1978)

Not often, but with surprising regularity, it happens that two biographers (or sometimes novelists) happen upon the same subject at the same time. Apart from the opening of an old archive or some obscure movement of the zeitgeist, quite why this should be isn't clear, and quite why it should happen in 1978, with Guyavitch, of all people, is even less so. But happen it did, and in Switzerland to boot.

Huggenberger and Jegerlehner had been promising young poets, but both had given way to mediocrity in middle age. Their rivalry remained undiminished, however, and was further in-

---

2 The reader of *Who's Who When Everyone Is Someone Else* will already have met her.

flamed when they discovered that each was working on a biography of a writer they each considered "theirs." The scarcity of material can only have aggravated matters.

When the books came out (on the same day), reviewers didn't know which to review, so reviewed neither. Only one attempted to review both books, but unfortunately mistook Huggenberger's for Jegerlehner's, and vice versa. Both books rapidly went out of print, and are now unobtainable.

The two biographers challenged each other to a knife fight, and—in the course of their duel—fell off the side of a small mountain near Lake Lucerne.

The Biographical Dictionary of Literary Failure, C. D. Rose, ed. (Melville House, 2014)

While it may seem somewhat gauche to recommend one's own work, I include this for two reasons. Firstly, to introduce the neophyte to the expanded field of study, and secondly, to acknowledge the question often asked of me: namely, why I hadn't included Guyavitch in the volume. (The answer being that having had several stories published, and some form of afterlife, Guyavitch was not eligible for the *Dictionary*'s strict selection criteria.)

The Guyavitch Heresy, Max Gate (William & Wilson, 1982)

Written in the style of a breathless thriller rather than a piece of literary scholarship, this would be a welcome addition to the occasionally over-arcane world of Guyavitch scholarship, were it not for the fact that it is complete rubbish. I include it here only to advise the reader not to bother with it.

Gate, a rare Englishman in the world of Guyavitch studies, here claims that Guyavitch did not really exist but was concocted by a group of writers as a means of promoting spurious nationalism via the creation of a literary heritage.[3] Members of the mysterious cabal behind this were all, according to Gate, later assassinated.

Gate's own provenance was later discovered to be questionable, and more interesting than this book. He was believed to have been a Soviet spy, but files recently released suggest that he was perhaps in the pay of the US Secret Services, informing both on the Soviets and the British. The reality is so confused, it is quite possible that Gate didn't quite know who he was informing on, or quite why. What is not in doubt is that he was channelling some major funding for ideologically approved cultural projects. Whether this was from the CIA directly or via a trans-global drug cartel has yet to be ascertained.

Gate later disappeared. His neatly folded clothes and parked car were found on a beach near Budleigh Salterton in 1986. No body was ever recovered.

The Guyavitch Fallacy, Marcel Mannbrotz (Bendrix and Bazakbal, 2018)

I once met Marcel Mannbrotz, and he was not amongst my admirers.[4] That said, this book is a trenchant and incisive look at much of the cant that surrounds the world of Guyavitch studies.

---

3   In a certain sense, their endeavour—whether real or not—was successful: I would be pleased to be a citizen of any nation in which Guyavitch were the notional national bard.

4   For more information, the reader is directed to my book *Who's Who When Everyone Is Someone Else,* pp. 164–171.

Mannbrotz thoroughly debunks not only Gate's book (mentioned above) but all the other pseudo-conspiracies and theories that surround Guyavitch and his work. Especial disdain is reserved for the acolytes and obsessives who see the work as infallible, as Mannbrotz notes the slipshod, patchwork quality of a number of the stories. Ultimately, however, his own combination of zeal and vitriol results in him being as blind to nuance and possibility as those as he accuses. What should be a refreshing cold glass of water, a sharp knife through the knots of humbug and sophistry, actually results in little more than further revelation of Mannbrotz himself, who remains an unpleasant, sneering character.

Candle Grease and Donkey Shit, Ostap Bender (Progress Publishing, 1962)

While Guyavitch's stories have often been said to possess cinematic qualities, few have noted their dramatic ones. This book, an account of a provincial touring theatre company in the late 1920s and early 1930s, includes one chapter that tells of an attempt to bring all of the nine stories to the stage. It was to be a kind of portmanteau performance, a whole evening in nine acts. An ensemble cast of two male and two female actors were to play all the parts. It was a brilliant idea. It was a disaster.

The tale of how it became so is brilliantly described by Bender in this book. Bender was the stagehand, props manager, lighting technician, and driver for the company, and he gives us his view, which manages to be both worm's eye and panoramic. "Candle Grease" and "Donkey Shit" are the nicknames given to the two company managers, a hustling couple of self-appointed theatrical entrepreneurs regarded with little but disdain by the actors they employ. The actors themselves come across as charming, learned, over-educated, under-employed, tender, needy, vain, selfish, brittle, and fraudulent, much like actors anywhere. Bender is a pitiless narrator, and so much the better for it.

Anastasiya Bok: A Life, Vanessa Portle (QUP, 2002)

The life of Bok (1885–1932) is here delicately retraced by Dr. Portle. Bok was a writer of fragments who published little during her lifetime and was soon forgotten. She had correspondences with Dagny Juel, Stanisława Przybyszewska, Anastasiya Mirovich, and Olga Preobrazhenskaia. The most tantalising note in this book is the suggestion that she may have collaborated with Ana Brac. I am including this book here due to the slight possibility that Bok was actually Guyavitch. I have contacted Portle to further discuss this, but she has consistently refused to reply to my queries.

Salt, Oil, Blood (Galleria Carlo di Marafia, 1998)

The catalogue for an exhibition of paintings and installations inspired by Guyavitch. Poorly printed, and with a brief text by Fausto Squattrinato (composed in International Art English, misinformed and deeply unenlightening), this is mostly of interest because it was what sparked my interest in Guyavitch.

The gallery was off a backstreet in Naples. How Guyavitch had ended up there, I do not know. The paintings were adequate, fine: I hardly remember them. But there was a wooden table, bare except for three iron bowls. One held salt, another oil, the third, blood.

Le Miroir Assombri de l'Amour, Claire Ligne (Hervé Frères, 1979)

A study of paraphilias in nineteenth-century French literature. While Ligne's reading of Baudelaire may be trite, her take on Verne is breathtaking. Mostly notable here for a mention of "Sosia and the Captain" in her discussion of the figure of the doppelgänger, which poses the question that when faced with our shadow-self, this premonitor of our end sent to fetch us, what else can we do but attempt to seduce them?

Maxim Guyavitch and the Defeated God, Simon Crubellier (Wiese & Pilaster, 2002)

In this book, Crubellier stakes the strange claim that Guyavitch was actually a member of the Protectors of the Word of God Defeated, and that all the stories (most notably, and inevitably, "Dead Johann") are an exegesis of their beliefs. The PWGD are a still-active heretical sect who maintain that when Lucifer and his rebel angels clashed with God, they were not vanquished. Lucifer won the battle, took the place of God, and remains there to this day. He has not been as destructive as some feared, instead proving to be indolent, chaotic, and capricious, given to short bursts of incredible malevolence and intense brutality mixed with longer bouts of casual laissez-faire cruelty, neglect, and injustice. The true God, meanwhile, has taken mortal form, and walks among us, unseen, unnoticed.

"Les fantômes de Guyavitch," Paul d'Aspremont (in *Contes et nouvelles*, Baldini, 1972)

A story in which the narrator reads all of Guyavitch's stories, and believes them all to be about ghosts, and himself—in turn—to be haunted by each of these ghosts. D'Aspremont was a minor French writer and critic who seems to have mysteriously vanished after writing this, his last story.

ACKNOWLEDGMENTS

AT THIS POINT, I fear, the reader may be growing weary of lists, so I will endeavour to be brief.

To all at Melville House for supporting this venture; to Nikolai Gogol, Isaac Babel, Franz Kafka, Bruno Schulz, Joseph Roth, Daniil Kharms, Walter Benjamin, and Robert Walser (and their translators) for building the world in which Guyavitch wrote; to Italo Calvino, Georges Perec, and Enrique Vila-Matas for furnishing it; to Andrew Gallix, Luke Kennard, Eley Williams, and all readers of the preceding volumes; to Jim Hinks, for a conversation at the Sandbar which led to my discovery of Guyavitch; to Fausto Squattrinato for his critical reading of early versions of this book, and to the manufacturers of Zapovit, who fuelled such criticisms; to the anonymous librarian who risked opening a cache of Guyavitch rarities for me; to everyone at the Hotel Terminus, for helping me to shelter from the angry mob of Guyavitch scholars that one night; to you the reader, for bearing with me this far, and trusting the tale; to the Guyavitchs yet to come; and to Dr Devereaux, for film knowledge, and more.